The Way I See It

Series by L.B. Tillit

Ozzie-Book 1

Zonta-Book 2

Blake-Book 3

Emma-Book 4

Emma

L.B. Tillit

MY EASY READ BOOKS

ISBN: 978-1-7352642-4-0
Published in the United States of America

Dedication

To all who dare to look inside themselves to find answers. And to those who help them make sense of it all.

Chapter 1

Out

"Emma? Where are you going?" My mother asked me in Mandarin. The Chinese language sounded like a soft song. She wasn't trying to challenge me. Not yet.

"Out," I answered in English as I gave her my best smile and grabbed my backpack purse. It had an over-the-top glossy-purple shine to it. But my mother wasn't looking at my purse. She was staring at my half-blue hair, which I'd partly pulled up into high ponytails. They looked more like horns than anything else. Most of my hair still hung down straight. I'd only added some blue color to my jet-black hair, but still, my mother wasn't happy. Which was good since *that* was my goal. But at that moment, I didn't want her to go off on me, so I shoved my hair over my shoulder.

"But where?" She suddenly switched to English. "You usually don't get out of bed until noon on Saturday." Her voice started to get louder. Any other day I might have told her. Normally, I didn't make such a big

deal, that is, *if* I'd been going to a friend's house or *if* I'd wanted to go shopping. But that Saturday was different! I was headed into Newport because I wanted to go to the final day of the State Wrestling Tournament at the Newport Coliseum. Blake Dockins, a white boy that I was into, was wrestling for Hancock High, and I wanted to surprise him. He'd won his match on Thursday night. Then he'd lost the semifinals round. But he texted me that he still had a chance at third place on Saturday. He didn't tell me *when* his match was. I hoped I wasn't going to be too late.

To be real, I should have asked him. It would have been a clear hint that I wanted to be there. But I didn't know if he was even picking up on all my other hints that I liked him. A lot! When Blake started to eat lunch with me two weeks before, I thought he liked me too. But then he backed off. I had smiled and winked at him so many times. I had even leaned into him when he let me. But it felt like he wasn't picking up on my flirting. I needed to give him a clear sign that I wanted to get to know him better. But going by myself into Newport was *not* something my mother would approve of, and chasing after a boy was even more of an issue.

"Just *out*, Ma." I tried to keep calm, but I really had a hard time. I grabbed my warm black jacket out of the closet. The one with the oversized hood that would pretty much cover my whole face if I wanted it to. Which I often did. No better way to hide from people that bothered me.

Just as I grabbed the handle to the front door, Ma yelled, "Stop, Emma!"

I stopped. But I didn't let go of the door handle, and I didn't look back at my mother. "What is it, Ma?"

"Look at me!" Ma commanded. I obeyed, slowly letting go of the door handle. I saw she already had her arms crossed, *and* she was shaking her head. "You do *not* speak to me this way. Your father and I have taught you better than this. Joseph never—"

"Joe is perfect! I know!" I began to pull on my jacket, punching my arms into the sleeves. My older brother was *always* the perfect one. He was smart and full of respect, all that my parents ever wanted. "Speaking of your *perfect* son, where is he?"

My mother's face went blank. "He . . . he . . . he said he's going—"

"Out." I finished her sentence since I had heard Joseph taking off only twenty minutes earlier. Ma had sent him off, yelling, *"Have a good time!"* By the look on Ma's face, I could tell she was finally making the connection.

"Okay." Ma dropped her eyes. Her voice softened as she returned to Mandarin. *"You're right. I just . . . worry about you."*

"Well, don't! I'll be fine!" I looked away.

3

"You'll be back for dinner, right? A special dinner tonight. Remember?" I was tired of Ma's special dinners. She always needed to celebrate some huge success. A special dinner when Joseph graduated with honors. A special dinner when Joseph was accepted to Hemby University, a top business school. I couldn't remember the last time we had a special dinner for me. I wanted to scream every time my parents gave my brother a special honor. I wanted Ma to know how awful it made me feel. But I kept my mouth shut.

That night's special dinner was because Tang-Lee Fabrics landed a big account. It was to supply fabric to be used to upgrade several Newport hotels. Blake's father had been part of that deal. Blake happened to be at our store that day. Food Time Grocery, where he worked, was Ma's last-minute backup to help cater some food. Blake had clearly been dragged along to help serve. His father, though, who was surprised to see Blake, had been a jerk to him that day. But still, that had nothing to do with business success. At least that night we were *not* focusing on Joseph, so I nodded and said, "I'll be back for dinner."

Ma nodded and finally left me alone. So I pulled the hood of my jacket up and let it slide halfway over my eyes as I opened the door and left.

Chapter 2

Transit

The first part was easy. I hopped on Bus 33 at the corner of 19th Street and Central Avenue. I was used to this bus. I'd always take it south to the middle of town and get off at the courthouse and cross Old Town Park to reach Tang-Lee Fabrics. I knew my father was already there that Saturday and that Ma would join him mid-morning. They tried to make the weekends a time to relax, but my family really didn't know what that meant. My parents worked really hard, and they expected Joseph and me to work as hard as they did. That was really their biggest push. We had to get good grades, be the best in school and get into a top college. We had to focus! School and grades came first, but there were times they pulled us in to help with the shop. Joseph helped more than I did, but I helped out on days when they needed an extra body. It helped me with spending money. But, to be real, it wasn't a set job like Blake had every weekend.

Although I fussed at Ma about Joseph being so perfect, he really was . . . at least compared to me. That was a problem because I was *far* from perfect. I knew I could *never* live up to their expectations, and they were beginning to see it too. But we never talked about it. Never.

My grades hadn't been good since middle school. Still, I did pass my classes, but most of them just barely. All the tricks I'd used in middle school stopped working once I hit high school, where it was just harder. History classes were the only classes that I cared about, and I made B's in them, which helped me keep an overall C average. All of this meant that I was in no honors classes. My parents hadn't said anything, but I knew they were let down. After all, they hadn't celebrated me or anything about me in a very long time.

My thoughts were starting to piss me off, so I pushed them away as Bus 33 reached the final stop. I waited for about fifteen minutes before I jumped onto Bus 21 to Newport. I had never done this before, but I kept looking at the map app on my phone to make sure I was headed the right way.

"Emma? Emma Tang-Lee? Is that you?" Someone called out from the back of the bus. I turned around to find Chastity Shaw making her way toward me. Her long, wavy brown hair hung over one shoulder in one long braid. Her short wool skirt seemed useless in the cold, even with her tall, brown knee-high boots. Her short, fuzzy brown jacket was the only real sign that it might still be winter. Only Chastity could get away with looking so good in the middle of winter. My mother would have had a cow if I had walked out of the house, winter or summer, looking like that. "Emma?" She had reached me, and I hadn't said a word. She had never talked to me before. Why now?

"Sorry. Hi." I smiled, sort of. The last thing I wanted was to spend time with Chastity Shaw.

Chapter 3

Chastity

"Where're you going?" Chastity asked as she plopped herself down across from me. Even though her clothes were great, I didn't care for Chastity's taste in make-up. She liked the bright colors that stood out against her pale, white skin. Not my cup of tea, but she liked it, so I didn't really care. Before I could answer, she added, "I'm headed to the State Wrestling Championship." My eyes went wide. She was known to hit on any boy she thought mattered. The fact was, she was pretty trashy. But she'd been with Owen Hemby for at least a month, a record for her. Chastity smiled at me. "I know, I know, you're wondering why I'm taking the bus." That wasn't what I was thinking at all. Still, she explained, "Well, my car is in the shop, and Daddy said there was no way he was driving me all the way to Newport to watch my boyfriend wrestle."

"But Owen isn't wrestling.'' I frowned since Owen hadn't made it to State. I explained, "Only Blake Dockins and Tank Jee are wrestling for Hancock High."

Chastity gave me a sly smile. "Yeah, but Daddy doesn't know that." I just stared at her, confused. She leaned in and whispered, "Owen is still there. You see, we always talk about doing it in the strangest—"

"Stop! Don't!" I looked out the window and watched Seaberg Avenue merge onto Hemby Highway. I was not looking forward to this very long, straight stretch. It had a ton of stops, so we had at least another thirty minutes.

"Aw, come on! Are you really such a prude?" Chastity leaned back and crossed her legs. Her skirt was so short that I was afraid her underwear would peek out.

I shook my head. "Just because I don't want to listen to your sleazy sex stories doesn't make me a prude."

Chastity lost her teasing smile. "Look, I was trying to be nice to you, but . . . whatever!" Suddenly, she stood up and headed to the back of the bus. I didn't really care. Better than listening to her go on about God-knows-what.

We finally reached Newport's transit station. It was almost ten by the time I headed down the walkway to catch the Newport Light Rail's A North. The modern tram had wide windows and a fancy blue streak along the outside, which made it look like a new form of transit. When the doors opened, I quickly hopped on the first light rail car that pulled up. I didn't even look to see if Chastity was following me.

I settled onto a cold bench and pulled out my phone, which had my ticket ready in case someone checked. Within seconds, Chastity plopped herself down across from me, again. This time she just crossed her arms as she stared at me. I tilted my head and sighed, "What?"

"So where are *you* going, Miss China?"

"Did you just call me *Miss China*?" My mouth stayed open in disbelief.

"Well, you sure as hell aren't Miss America, but you're acting like it . . . so Miss—"

"I'm American. Get it right!" I held her glare.

She looked away. "Okay. Sorry. Guess that was sort of—"

"Racist!" I finished for her.

Chastity unlocked her arms and waved her hand in the air. "A little over the top, don't you think? Stereotyping, maybe, but racist? Really?" I just glared at her until she added, "Can we move on. I'm sorry, okay?"

I watched some people across from us begin to stare. I rolled my eyes and sighed again. "Okay, whatever."

10

A few minutes of silence passed. Only a few. "So where are you going? I bet you're headed to the same place I am." When I didn't answer, she shoved my knee. "Right?" I gave in and nodded. "I knew it!" That sly smile returned. "I bet you got your eye on some boy. Wait! Not Tank . . . it's that freak, Blake!"

I looked at her again and frowned. Again. "He's not a freak. What's wrong with you?"

"Nothing's wrong with me." Chastity leaned in again. "But I tell you, be careful with that one. I was nice to him one time, and then he crushed on me. Hard. Stared at me all the time. Freaked me out!"

"He has autism. Okay?" I couldn't help myself. "He doesn't always know what to say or do, but he's a nice guy."

Chastity grinned. "I knew it. It *is* Blake!" I rolled my eyes. It was like Chastity only heard what she wanted to hear.

"Maybe." I gave her a little something so she would drop it. "Not too sure yet if he likes me back." I dropped my eyes to stare at the smudge on her boot before I added, "Not that it really matters to you."

Chastity crossed her legs again, but thankfully she pulled her skirt down as well. She ignored my dig at her. Her voice became all sweet. "Come on. Who wouldn't crush on Miss China!" I glanced up at her face. She was grinning, hoping I'd catch her tease.

11

I rolled my eyes again and let it go. I could keep fighting her. I was good at fighting and liked to sass people who deserved it. To be real, maybe even to some people who didn't deserve it. But I couldn't talk about what I really felt. Like at that moment, I had no words to tell Chastity that I hated her calling me Miss China, not because she was stereotyping me. But because it reminded me how much I *wasn't* Miss China. I fell short of all the traits that made me worthy of the name. Except for how I looked. My best bet was to ignore Chastity's comments and focus on Blake.

But thinking about Blake wasn't easy either. As I watched the ever-changing backdrop at the platforms of each station pass by, I began to wonder, for the first time, what the heck I was doing? I knew nothing about wrestling, and for all I knew, Blake could already be done wrestling. I hadn't even thought through what I'd say when I saw him. Up to that point, I had failed to get the message across to him about how I felt. What made me think showing up would be any different?

14th street was my . . . our stop. We exited the light rail and were surprised to be met by a soft snow flurry. As we headed to the towering coliseum only a block away, I lifted my hood up over my head to keep the cool snowy breeze from freezing my ears and nose. Chastity zipped up her small jacket and fussed the whole time about how cold she was.

We walked up to the huge building with at least ten doors spread across the front, mostly for those huge concerts or pro-sports events. But that day, it was just the two of us that walked through one of the doors and up to the only open ticket window to pay our entrance fee. Inside, there were suddenly several people coming from all directions. Pouring in and out of several hallways, they were talking and buying food at a handful of open concession stands. We weren't sure which hallway to take, so we walked to the closest one that led us into the coliseum.

It wasn't like our gym at all, except the smell was close, just not as strong. We were looking down on bleachers that dipped toward the wide coliseum floor. The entire floor was covered by what looked like one huge blue mat with ten wrestling circles evenly placed across the whole space. It looked like an organized mess. Whistles blew while fans screamed, booed, and cheered all at the same time. I thought that it was worse than a three-ring circus. It was more like a ten-ring circus! For real!

I looked up and found a whole other level of seats that shot up the sides of the walls, but they were all empty. It looked like the tournament was only on the lower level. Still, I was not sure how we would find anyone in this mess. Chastity checked a message on her phone. Suddenly, she looked down the bleachers to the far right and spotted Owen waving at her. She glanced at me. "Gotta go!" I nodded once and watched her unzip her jacket to let it hang over her shoulders.

I sighed again and hoped the trip would be worth it.

Chapter 4

Fans

I leaned on the metal railing not far from where I came in. As I looked down on all the activity, I was trying to spot Blake. But everyone looked the same to me, especially with all the team colors and caps. I had watched Chastity as she looped her way down and around the mess and found members of Hancock High's wrestling team. She'd made herself comfortable next to Owen, who was busy screaming at someone on the mat nearby. It might have been Tank, based on the very large size of the wrestlers shifting and shoving, each trying to take the other one down. But maybe not. Clearly, Chastity would need to wait for Owen to be more focused on her than wrestling. I chuckled to myself. Chastity was too much!

"What's so funny?" Someone came up next to me. I was surprised when I turned to find Ozzie Waxman. He had a brace strapped to his knee, two drinks in his hands, and his faithful Cleveland Browns cap on his head.

I looked up at him as he towered over me. "Um, what?" I was confused why Ozzie was talking to me. First Chastity, and now Ozzie? Then I remembered I sat with Blake and Ozzie for a few days at lunch before Blake started eating with my friends and me. Ozzie was a huge black guy that I sort of knew. To be real, I mostly saw him as an All-American jock with a football career ahead of him. Except he tore his ACL last fall and was still recovering from the surgery. Rumor was that he tried to take some pills to end it all, but I didn't believe it. I blew it off as one of those sick rumors to screw around with a person. He was way too nice, and he really seemed to have it together. He even stuck up for Blake when the rest of the jocks turned their back on him. No one with a death wish could be that strong!

Ozzie smiled. "You were just laughing to yourself."

"Oh, that!" I smiled a little. "I was thinking about how Chastity is just too much!" I pointed to where she was sitting. She looked like she was checking her phone, clearly bored.

Ozzie nodded. "Yes, that's one way to put it." When I didn't say anything else, Ozzie asked, "What're you doing here?"

I frowned up at him. "Why do *you* care?" Ozzie lifted his eyebrows, surprised at my response. But what was I supposed to say? *Oh, I'm hoping to spill my feelings out to Blake today?* The look on Ozzie's face told me I had chosen the wrong response, no matter what the truth was. I shook my head at myself. "Sorry. I didn't mean to sound so—"

"Angry," Ozzie finished.

I shook my head and argued, "No, I was thinking more like *uptight*." He nodded but didn't say anything back. He took a sip out of one of the cups. I could feel him shift next to me, clearly ready to leave me. "I'm here to see Blake." I blurted out, but I felt stupid.

"Me too." Ozzie's smile was back. "After all the crap he went through with Carlos this season, Blake has earned some serious backing." He pointed to the bleachers where Chastity was making another attempt to get Owen's attention. "Looks like Hancock turned out to cheer. He's got a chance at third place!"

"I heard." I nodded. I stared at the bleachers and realized that there were several other faces I recognized. Zonta Jones, a biracial girl from school, was the first face to stand out. There was no denying it, she was beautiful, and she knew it. She had perfect light brown skin and brown hair with just the right number of curls, which were perfectly styled. Then there was that innocent look that I didn't buy for a second. To me, she always seemed a little trashy. I'd heard rumors that she and Ozzie had hooked up right before they broke up. Yet, somehow, they were friends? It just seemed so wrong. But I felt a little bad for thinking that way, especially since she had been assaulted by Carlos a few weeks earlier. Thanks to Blake, she got away without being badly hurt. Still, she just bothered me.

Imani Grace sat next to her. I always thought she was some shy black girl, but I'd heard she was a pretty cool wrestler herself. I learned quickly that she wasn't shy, but she only talked when she had something to say. Her best friend, Summer, was next to her. She was so sure of herself that she had no problem showing up in a full-on purple body suit. She'd stated more than one time in a day, "I'm big, black, and beautiful, so deal with it!" On the other side of her, Mary Ann Daniels, a tall skinny white girl who was new to the school, was laughing at whatever Summer had just said. Imani, Summer, and Mary Ann sat with us at lunch some days. They were friends with my best friend, Billy Seaberg, since they were all into the arts.

Billy was white too. My parents had asked me why I didn't have more Asian friends. Those words always hit me hard. They had no clue that the smart Asian kids, as well as any smart white, black, Indian, or biracial friends I had made in elementary school, were all in advanced classes. Only a few were stuck up. Mostly everyone was just busy and focused on their own world. Once in a while, I'd have classes with other Asians, like Tank Jee. But he was Korean American and was a popular jock. Still, we had nothing in common, either. The fact was that he was a star wrestler, which meant he brought his family honor. But me? I brought nothing to the Tang-Lee honor table, but I could never explain all this to my parents. There was no way they would understand, so I didn't try. Instead, I told them that Billy was good enough. One best friend was enough.

I had asked Billy to come with me, but he said he was not going to spend his day watching jocks wrestle. I was on my own. I looked up at Ozzie. "I thought it was mostly the team that would show up."

"Nope, a bunch of us are here. You can come sit with us." He looked at me and shrugged his shoulders. "Unless you want to stand up here and throw shade at the next person trying to be nice to you." It was weird hearing Ozzie tease me, but I knew he wasn't a jerk like so many of the other jocks. I knew he was being real.

"Very funny." I stuck out my tongue like a little girl. But I quickly transformed it into a real smile.

Ozzie shook his head at me as I followed him down the concrete steps. The energy and noise became more intense with each level as he led me to Hancock High's section of the bleachers.

I was grateful for about two minutes. As we approached the group, I quickly became annoyed. I realized a little too late that we were going to sit *with* Zonta. I reached up and touched the side of my head. A dull ache began to build.

19

Chapter 5

Surprise!

"Hi, Emma?" Zonta smiled up at me, but before I could say anything, Ozzie handed her the second drink. "Thanks, Ozzie!" Ozzie dug into his jeans pocket and handed Zonta some coins and a few dollars.

"That should be the right change." Ozzie pointed out as he took a sip of his drink.

Without counting the change, Zonta smiled as she shoved the change into the pocket of her black jacket. A jacket that was a perfect fit, not big and bulky like mine. "Now I don't have to die of thirst," she laughed as she knocked Ozzie's shoulder as he settled in next to her. There *was* a seat in-between them. Still, he was close enough. Did she have to flirt with everyone? At least she didn't flirt with Blake. But she did flirt with my brother, and that was not okay with me. Joseph didn't talk much about Zonta after he tutored her on Tuesdays and Thursdays for her SATs. Still, there was a look on his face that told me he was falling for her. "Are you okay?" Zonta broke into my thoughts.

"What?" I nodded and dropped my hand from my head. "Yes, I'm good. Why?"

"Looked like you were about to bite my head off." Zonta tried to smile, but it was more like an upside-down frown.

"Oh, that?" I forced a laugh. "I was just thinking about someone. Sorry."

Zonta dropped her shoulders, and a real smile spread across her face. "Good. I sure wouldn't want to be that person!"

"Me either." Ozzie jumped in as I forced another laugh. Ozzie added, "Well, are you going to sit down?"

There was no room on the other side of Ozzie. Imani, Summer, and Mary Ann were sitting there, and Imani looked like she was explaining wrestling to her friends. There was no way I was going to try to squeeze into the seat between Zonta and Ozzie, and I really, *really* did not want to spend my day next to Zonta. The dull throb in my head began to build. I scanned the seats in front of them and behind them, hoping for anyone else I could use as an excuse to choose a different spot.

"Emma?" A familiar voice came from behind. I felt relief rush through my body as I turned to face Blake. He was wearing a black warm-up jacket and sweats. His blond hair was messed up, but his

21

crystal blue eyes were looking right at me. It was not something many people got a chance to really see for very long. They were so intense that it took me longer than normal to find my words.

"Hi, Blake! Surprise!" I finally said, but it fell flat. I felt stupid as I watched Blake drop his eyes.

"You came to watch me wrestle?" His voice was straightforward. He was making sure he understood me.

"Yes! I came to watch you." I smiled as he looked up at me and let his eyes lock with mine for as long as he could handle. He looked up at my high ponytails, which he told me once that he liked. Then he looked right at me again as he asked, "Why?"

It was my chance to be straight with him and tell him that I liked him as more than friends, but I knew Zonta was right behind me listening in. No way would I let her have any insight into my world! So I pointed at Zonta and the others, and I tried to sound like it was no big deal. "They came too! Can't we all come and support Hancock High's best wrestlers?" I bit my lip and hoped he didn't take it the wrong way.

Blake's eyes flickered. It wasn't the answer he had hoped for. It wasn't the answer I had wanted to give. Suddenly my headache hit me full force. I closed my eyes and reached up and rubbed my temple, hoping the pain would go away. The noise and whistles didn't help any. "Are you okay?" Blake asked.

I opened my eyes and tried to smile. "Yeah. I just got a bad headache." Suddenly, I realized that was my way to move somewhere else. I turned to face Zonta and Ozzie. I was surprised to find they weren't looking at us at all. "Listen. I'm going to sit somewhere higher up where it's not as loud. Got a headache."

Ozzie was already focused on the wrestling match closest by and didn't hear me, and Zonta looked up at me and smiled. "Okay. Hope you feel better." Then she turned and watched the match as well.

As I turned back to face Blake, he turned away from me. "Hey, wait!" I grabbed his arm. Which was a mistake. He pulled away quickly but caught himself and relaxed it again. "Sorry, I didn't mean to—"

"No big deal." Blake smiled. "I'm still working on letting people I like touch me." Then he dropped his eyes.

But I smiled. "People you like?" The throb in my temple let up a little. I needed to grab my headache pills, but I didn't want Blake to think I wasn't listening to him. The pills could wait.

Blake took a deep breath and looked at me again. "Yes, people like you."

I smiled really big and reached out to touch his arm again. He let me and smiled back. That was my chance. "That makes two of us." I leaned in just a little. "Because I don't touch people I don't like."

It only took a second for him to put two and two together before his smile grew. I was suddenly so excited. He got it. He finally got my message. And I could see that I hadn't been wrong. He liked me too. It was a breakthrough, for sure.

"BLAKE!" Coach Miller was standing facing us from a few bleachers down. "Get warmed up!"

"Got to go!" Blake was still smiling at me.

"I'll be watching." I smiled back. As Blake took off down the steps, I saw Coach Miller glance at me, at Blake, and back at me. He shook his head. My eyes went wide as I felt the throb in my head scream for meds. Coach wasn't happy I had gotten into Blake's head. He didn't need anything else except to focus on this match. I suddenly felt so stupid and hoped I hadn't made a huge mistake in showing up.

Chapter 6

Perfect Seat?

I moved as quickly as I could away from the area where most of the Hancock High fans were sitting and climbed halfway back up the lower level of the coliseum. I had to find the perfect seat, since I didn't want to look pitiful sitting alone so far away. I needed to sit far enough away for the noise to let up a little but close enough to still see what was going on. And, there still needed to be some people.

I spotted an empty seat near a skinny, blond white woman and a young blond girl that looked like her daughter. The girl was busy coloring something. They were both dressed nicely and looked like they'd just come from a mother-daughter photo shoot for the latest winter fashion. They seemed harmless enough, so I moved into a spot two seats away. As I sat down, the girl looked up at me and smiled. She had beautiful brown eyes, and she looked a little familiar. I pretended that a whistle had grabbed my attention as I focused on the movement in the closest wrestling circle. I didn't want these people to think I was being rude. But when I glanced over again, the girl was still staring at me. She kept staring at me, and when I looked at her a third time, she finally said, "Hi."

"Hi." I nodded and looked away again.

"Do you like to color?" The little girl jumped out of her seat and scooted over to me. I was surprised she wasn't holding a children's coloring book. It was one of those really complex adult coloring books. She was almost finished with a detailed scene made up of flowers and birds. It was perfectly colored and made me want to step into that world.

"Penny!" The lady jumped up and walked over to grab her child's arm. "We don't talk to people we don't know." The lady looked at me. "I am so sorry she's bothering you. She's only eight." Her blue eyes had dark shadows underneath them, and her blond hair was pulled back in a messy bun.

"Ma'am, it's not a problem. Really." I smiled and meant it.

"Mom! I *do* know her!" Penny pulled her arm away from her mother. "If you would pay attention!" What child used language like that? I thought the woman would lose it. My mother would have pulled me out of the building and grounded me for a week for talking back in public. She pointed at my face. "Look at her! See?"

26

The woman took a deep breath and smiled at me awkwardly. "I'm so sorry. Penny doesn't always know when to—" The lady's eyes quickly focused on me. "Wait! You're . . . Ellen . . . no Emily . . ."

"Emma, Mom! Emma!" Penny said my name like I had known her my whole life.

I searched their faces, and even though there was something familiar, I just couldn't figure it out. "Excuse me, but do I know you from somewhere?"

Penny giggled. "Blake has your picture as his backdrop on his phone."

I felt my cheeks warm. "He does? How do you know this?"

"He's my brother!"

Chapter 7

Penny

My cheeks grew very warm. It was Blake's family! What were the odds I'd sit next to Blake's family? Then I realized that it *was* the state championship, so the odds were good. I hadn't even thought about his family. Not at all. But there I was, sitting next to his sister and his mother, who were looking at me like I was a part of their family. I had just told Blake, only five minutes earlier, that I really liked him. My temple began to throb again. "Oh . . . nice to meet you." The smile that had come easily a few minutes earlier was suddenly hard to pull off.

"Oh, no!" Penny's smile dropped.

"What?" Her mother asked.

She pointed at my face. "She doesn't mean it."

I shook my throbbing head and smiled at Penny. "Yes . . . yes, I do." I rubbed my temple and looked up at her mother. "I'm sorry, ma'am, it's just that my head is killing me."

"Don't be sorry." Blake's mother waved her hand at me. "I get headaches all the time." She moved back to her seat and sat down.

Penny reached for my hand that was gripping the arm of my seat. "Well, scoot over and drink something." I let her pull me out of my seat to settle in the one next to her. Penny's mother, who had already settled back into her seat, pulled a water bottle out of a large bag. It looked like a purse, but as I touched the cold bottle, I guessed the purse doubled as a cooler.

"Thank you, Mrs. Dockins," I said as I reached into my glossy purple backpack purse and pulled out some headache pills.

"You're welcome." The blond woman smiled. I could see Blake in her eyes. "But I'm not Mrs. Dockins and I never have been. I'm Ashley Long-Hunt, but you can call me Ashley." I could never call her Ashley. My mother would be furious. But I didn't want to call her Ms. Long-Hunt. That would upset her. I decided I wouldn't call her anything since I wouldn't be there that long anyway.

"I'm Penny Long-Hunt." Penny smiled at me. "Blake's got a different daddy."

I remembered the man who had been a jerk to Blake three weeks earlier when Blake had helped Food Time Grocery cater the food for Tang-Lee Fabrics. His father, Mr. Cole P. Dockins, was the same man who was a part of the big account that my parents landed. The one we were celebrating with a special dinner that night. "Yes, that's right. I've met him."

Ms. Long-Hunt frowned. "Really?"

"Yes, ma'am. He's a client of Tang-Lee fabrics. My parents own the store."

Ms. Long-Hunt looked away. "Oh, yeah. Blake told us." Blake's mother pretended to be paying attention to the wrestling taking place on every mat spread across the coliseum floor. But her eyes stared blankly at one spot.

I wanted to be clear that although Mr. Cole P. Dockins was a client of my parents, it didn't mean I had any loyalty toward the man. "Ma'am, I saw him talk to Blake at our store. And he was a total jerk." I looked at Penny's big eyes. "Sorry . . . I mean, he was *not* nice."

Ms. Long-Hunt suddenly turned and looked at me again, a huge smile spread across her face. "Trust me, she's heard me call him worse." I had been right. She needed to hear that I was on her side, not his. She looked back out at the mats, this time really searching for Blake.

Penny leaned into me and whispered, "I'll tell you later."

Later? Did they expect me to hang out with them all day? Penny started drawing again, and I could feel the medicine begin to ease my headache some. The little girl looked up at me. "I think you should color with me."

"Excuse me?"

"You could use a little therapy." She smiled. What in the world was she talking about? And since when did a child talk about therapy? When Penny saw me tilt my head, trying to figure her out, she flipped her book to show me the cover. *Coloring Therapy*. "See! Want to give it a try?"

I smiled at Penny. To be real, I didn't like little kids much, but Penny was something else. *And* it was way better than sitting next to Zonta. "Sure!" I said as I grabbed a green pencil, found a corner section with grass, and started coloring. "But it might be like trying to grow a unicorn horn."

Penny giggled. "What does that mean?"

I didn't look up as I finished coloring the first little square. "You know, like trying to make the impossible happen."

Penny giggled again. "I'll have you know I dressed up as a unicorn last Halloween. So trust me, it *is* possible!"

Chapter 8

First Time

"Look! It's Blake! It's his turn." Ms. Long-Hunt patted Penny's leg. Penny and I both looked up from the almost-complete page full of color. Penny had been right. I'm not so sure how long we'd been coloring in silence, but my headache was completely gone. We scanned the area where Ms. Long-Hunt was pointing until we found Blake. He took his place in the middle of one of the ten wrestling circles closest to us. The referee was talking to some people on the sidelines while the two wrestlers waited. I knew the wrestlers wore these one-piece uniforms, but seeing Blake in one was a whole other thing. The black material stretched tightly across all his muscles. Nothing was hidden. I swallowed as I felt my cheeks warm.

"Aren't those onesies a little tight?" My eyes opened wide. Had I really just asked that out loud? I was sitting next to his little sister and his mother! How embarrassing!

I heard Penny laugh at me, so I turned and found her mother still looking at her son. I was lucky there was too much noise for her to hear my comment. But Penny had heard. "They're not called onesies! They're *singlets*." She was happy to fill me in. "They have to be tight, or else they could get all twisted up in the singlet and not focus on the moves. He's got to get the other guy pinned to the mat to have a win, and we don't want clothes to get in the way of a pin. Get it?"

I nodded at her and smiled. "Got it." She didn't have a clue about why I thought the singlets were too tight. Thank God she was only eight! I couldn't help but watch every muscle flex as Blake kept moving around, waiting for the referee to start the match.

"GO, BLAKE!" Penny stood up and yelled, jarring me out of my focus on Blake's flexing muscles. Ms. Long-Hunt stood up, too, and crossed her arms across her chest. Her stare became so fixed on her son that I thought she might pass out.

I quickly reminded myself that I came to support Blake, not stare at him! So I jumped up and yelled, "YOU GOT THIS, BLAKE!" There was so much yelling and noise that I was sure Blake didn't hear us at all. After the look Coach Miller had given me, I thought maybe that was a good thing.

Penny looked up at me and grinned. "This is so exciting. It's the first time this year we get to see him wrestle."

"What do you mean?" I looked down at her. Hadn't they been to most of his matches like other parents? I tilted my head, trying to figure out why.

Penny read me, again. "Mom works all the time, so we usually don't get to go. My brother Kyle couldn't come today because he's off with some special Marine-group-thing that he's part of." Penny looked down at Blake. "Isn't it exciting?"

I smiled. "Yes, it is! It's my first time too!"

"Look!" Ms. Long-Hunt unlocked her arms for a second and pointed at the movement on the mat. The match had begun.

Chapter 9

Third Place

Blake and his opponent were moving around the mat in a circle. Suddenly, they charged each other. I had never realized how intense wrestling was. It was like nothing I'd ever seen. I watched as Blake reached for the other guy's leg. Just as he had a grip, trying to pull him off balance, the other guy shifted, causing Blake to stumble. Blake quickly got his footing, but the other guy had one hand around the back of Blake's neck. Blake's hand swung up and gripped the guy's neck as well. They were locked head-against-head as their other hands swung around, trying to get a grip on some other body part.

I was a little confused with Blake. Not the wrestling. But Blake. He hated to be touched. How could he stand this? I wanted to ask Penny, but maybe she didn't know that I knew that Blake had autism. And I didn't want to upset Blake by talking to them about it. It had only been a few weeks since he had shared his "secret," although most of us knew that something was up. Still, it had taken guts for him to tell us. I didn't want to push it.

Within seconds Blake was on top of the other guy with his whole body trying to press the guy into the mat for a pin. The other guy kept pushing with his legs until he scooted them out of the big circle. The whistle blew, and they both had to start in the circle again. The other guy was on his hands and knees in the middle of the circle. Blake came in from behind, took a knee, and with one hand on the guy's elbow, he reached his other arm around the guy's waist. As soon as the ref gave the signal, the bottom guy jumped up and broke free. I wasn't quite sure what was happening. A scoreboard showed the guy had a few points, but Blake had some points too. With all the changing back and forth, I didn't get what earned points and what didn't. I watched the back and forth as the two kept scoring points on each other. Before I knew it, they were in the third period.

"Oh, no!" Penny cried.

"What's wrong?" I asked as I glanced down at her.

"Blake is a point behind."

I frowned. "I'm sure it's fine. He'll get more points."

She grabbed my arm. "You don't understand. There are only three periods and the other guy just has to keep Blake from scoring. It means he JUST has to hold him."

I looked down at Blake, who was trying to get a grip on the other guy. He was desperate to score. He lunged for the guy's legs, but the guy shot both of his legs backward and landed on top of Blake. The guy spread out his legs as he spun himself around to keep Blake face down on the mat. Right away, some more points showed up on the board. The other team yelled, "Hold him! Hold him!"

Blake's feet tried to wrap around the back of the guy's legs, but as he began to move the guy off him, the whistle blew. The match was over. Just like that, Blake had lost his chance at third place.

Chapter 10

Blame

My stomach dropped as I watched Blake walk off the mat. Coach Miller shook his hand and patted his back, but that took less than three seconds. Blake hung his head and walked over to a pile of clothes a few feet away. As he zipped up his warm-up jacket, he looked up at us. It took me a second to realize he was *not* looking at me. He was looking at his mother. There was a look in Blake's eyes that hit me hard. I knew that feeling and I knew it well. He felt like a failure when all he wanted was to please his mother. To be real, if I hadn't already had a lockdown on my emotions, I would have burst into tears. But I didn't. I didn't even look at Penny or Ms. Long-Hunt. I knew I wouldn't have been able to handle the looks on their faces either. Instead, I swallowed hard and pushed a smile to my face as I reached up and waved.

My wave worked. Blake spotted me, and his broken look turned into a smile as he waved back. Suddenly, Coach Miller's head turned to see who Blake was waving at. He frowned and walked right up to Blake. He said something that made Blake's face scrunch up. It was the same look he always made when he didn't understand something. He started shaking his head as he spoke back to Coach, but Coach waved his hand up at me and then at the mat. Blake glanced in my direction and then away again, still shaking his head at his coach.

"What's going on, Mom?" I heard Penny ask.

I turned and watched Ms. Long-Hunt shake her head. "I don't know, baby. But that Coach better stop yelling at my boy! He did the best he could. What's his problem?"

"Excuse me, ma'am. I think it's me," I said, and the two of them turned to look at me. When they kept staring, I added, "The coach thinks because I'm here, Blake has his mind on me, not the match."

"That doesn't make sense." Ms. Long-Hunt said. I was thankful she didn't ask me why or if we were a couple. But I didn't understand her response. She stared down at her son, who was still arguing with Coach. "That doesn't sound like Blake."

"But, ma'am . . . I basically told him I liked him too . . . right before I came up here." I confessed. I felt *so* stupid. Who talks to a boy's mother *and* little sister about this stuff? What was wrong with me? Still, I felt like I was somehow to blame.

Penny giggled. "That's so sweet."

Ms. Long-Hunt looked at me and smiled just a little. "I guess there was something good that came from Blake blabbing his secrets." My eyebrows shot up. It wasn't what I expected her to say. Then she narrowed her eyes and asked, "But did you like him before you knew . . . you know . . . about him . . .?"

"Yes, ma'am." I stopped her from saying what was obviously hard for her to say. "Well, not at the beginning of the year. But he started to grow on me." I couldn't believe I was trying to explain any feelings I had toward Blake. To his *mother*! I could never explain my feelings to anyone, but there I was, trying to convince Blake's mom that knowing about Blake's autism didn't play a role. In truth, I didn't really know how much I liked him. Still, it seemed the right thing to say at that moment.

Ms. Long-Hunt took a deep breath. "I'm only curious since I thought it should stay a secret. Clearly, I was wrong." She sighed, "Something I have to get used to." She looked at me and frowned. "But still, it doesn't make sense that he would focus on you and not the match."

I looked down at Blake, who stopped arguing and walked over to grab his water bottle. He was still shaking his head when I looked back at his mother. I had to ask. "Excuse me, but why do you think that?"

Ms. Long-Hunt sighed. "Because he's *always* got you in his head. Today is not any different."

Chapter 11

What Now?

I didn't know what to say, so I didn't say anything. What did *got you always in his head* even mean? I knew he liked me, but that was a pretty intense statement. Chastity's words from earlier hit me. *Then he crushed on me . . . hard . . . freaked me out.* I pushed the thought away since that was not how he was acting toward me. He was not freaking me out. His mother was.

"Excuse me, I think I'm going to go now." I stood up and forced a smile. It was all just too much! "Maybe I can talk to Blake before I head home."

"Nice to meet you, Emma." Penny shoved out her hand, and I shook it.

Ms. Long-Hunt nodded in my direction. "Please tell Blake to come up here. I want to understand what's going on. Are we done or what?"

I nodded back and grabbed my backpack purse. I hurried down the concrete steps, passed Zonta and Ozzie's row, and headed straight for

Blake. I hoped talking to Blake would help me get his mother's words out of my head. I didn't believe finding out about Blake's autism had anything to do with me liking him, and I wanted to prove to myself that he wasn't someone with a hard crush on me. Someone I needed to worry about. But, to be real, I was mostly worried that I had ruined the match for him. What if he had been so focused on me that he messed up? I found him chugging his water off to the side, close to the stadium wall, away from the bleachers. A few other wrestlers, all in different colored singlets and warm-ups, leaned up against the wall watching the matches still taking place in all ten circles. When one was done, it was only minutes before the next match took place.

"Blake?" I reached him as he shoved the lid back down on his bottle.

He looked at me and smiled. "Emma. Hi." His smile faded a little as he looked back down at his bottle. "Sorry I lost the match."

"No, I'm sorry," I said out loud, ready to point out that it was all my fault. I felt so bad and didn't believe his mom knew what she was talking about. I was to blame!

Blake glanced back up at me. "What are you talking about?"

"I saw how Coach was yelling at you and pointing at me. I think I shouldn't have come at all. You might have won. I heard 3rd place is a big deal and helps with schools, but I ruined that for you and—"

"No, you didn't." He pointed toward the mats, where other matches were still going on. "You didn't mess me up at all. I didn't think of you at all when I was wrestling."

"Oh." This time I looked down at my feet. Part of me felt embarrassed. The other part of me hurt. A few minutes earlier, I believed it was somehow messed-up that he was thinking of me all the time. Suddenly, I'm not okay with him *not* thinking of me. What was wrong with me? I looked up at his blue eyes. He was trying to read me by taking in every detail. I didn't want him to see my own confusion, so I added, "Then what did Coach say to you?"

Blake dropped his eyes and smiled. "Exactly what you said."

I laughed out loud and slapped his arm. He let me, without flinching. "So. What did you say to him?"

Blake looked up, and his head turned. He frowned as he settled his gaze on his mother and Penny. "I told him it wasn't you. It was them. I wanted so bad for Mom to see me win. She supports me by working all the time so I can do this. I just wanted her to see it was worth it."

I looked up at Ms. Long-Hunt, who was now coloring with Penny. I didn't really know them, but there was one thing I did know. "Well, she's very proud of you and told me she thought you did your best. I thought she was going to come down here and give Coach Miller a piece of her mind if he didn't stop fussing at you!"

43

"For real?" Blake laughed and glanced at me a second before he looked back up into the bleachers.

"For real." I smiled as I watched Blake's frown melt away. "She wants you to get up there and talk to her as soon as you can."

"I just got to grab my stuff, and I'll head up there."

Before he moved, I asked, "So, is that it for you today?"

He smiled. "No way. I still got a shot at fifth place. Colleges are all about the top six at State." I felt such relief. Not only wasn't I to blame, but he still had a chance of finishing at the top, where it mattered. His blue eyes stared right into mine. "Are you staying?"

I held his gaze. "I wouldn't miss it!"

Chapter 12

Truth

When I told Blake I wouldn't miss his chance at 5th place, I had no idea what I was getting myself into. How long could it really be before he wrestled again? I didn't realize he had to wrestle two more matches. One to get a chance at 5th place and then, finally, the match for 5th place. Even that didn't seem bad at first, but then it turned out that the first match wasn't until 2 p.m., and then IF he won, the final match would be late afternoon or early evening. It would depend on how all the matches played out.

That meant that I spent a lot of time coloring with Penny. We had to start a new page full of fish and seashells. A bunch of times, I jumped up and got Blake to walk around to get food with me, even if it meant Ozzie and the others joined us. Anything to break up the slow pace.

I took a ton of pics and texted Billy throughout the day. He'd respond with a ton of emojis. Somehow, in the middle of all our back and forth, I left out that I knew Blake was really into me or that I had told him that I really liked him too! Billy knew I'd been flirting in my own way, but he thought I was trying to be kind . . . be a friend . . . make Blake feel good about himself. But I hadn't told Billy the whole story. I wasn't sure why I hadn't told him that I liked Blake. I'd told myself that it was no big deal *and* that Billy would be okay with me telling him later. After all, he was my best friend.

But as the day dragged on, it wasn't fun texting him anymore. I felt like I was keeping something from him. Which I was. So I decided to stop texting Billy. But because we were best friends, I would let him know.

lots going on. can't text. ttyl

has something changed???

I looked at Billy's response. Why couldn't he just answer that he'd talk to me later too?

nope. just want to chill. take it all in.

As soon as I sent the text, I realized it sounded really lame. I never wanted to take anything in without texting Billy all about it. Maybe he would let it go.

k. whatever. ttyl

Whatever? Was he pissed? I read over his response three times before I decided that Billy would get over it. I shoved my phone in my purse and forced myself to stop thinking about Billy.

I was happy for Blake and his family when he won the match that gave him a shot at 5th place, but when I found out that the final match was not until 6 p.m., I knew I was screwed. Ma would be so mad at me for being late for dinner. It wasn't like we ate together often, but I had told her that morning that I would be there at the special dinner.

I thought about leaving, but Blake was so happy, and winning 5th place would be a big deal for Blake and Hancock High. At 5 p.m. I finally texted my mother.

i'll be late

It only took my mother a few seconds to respond back.

Why?

out later than i thought

Where are you?

I'd been gone all day and knew she was sick worrying about where I was. I really didn't want her to know. But I REALLY didn't want to be grounded. Not when I was starting something with Blake. Whatever that something was! It would suck big-time if I couldn't be with him for a month, since a month was my mother's go-to punishment. I

47

looked at Blake, who was sitting next to Penny, talking and laughing. Suddenly, I had an idea.

im at state wrestling tournament in newport for my friend blake. rmr the boy blake? his dad is mr dockins. hes going 2 try 2 win 5th place. big honor 4 hancock.

I took a deep breath and waited. I stared at my screen. I had taken a chance telling the truth. But I also had left a lot of room for my mother to fill in any key facts. The whole truth was that Blake's father was not at the coliseum and not in Blake's life. But my mother really didn't know any of that. Sure, she'd shown surprise that Mr. Dockins had a son and found his response to her at the store odd. He'd referred to Blake as a result of *young love* that led to an *unplanned baby*. But Ma was only focused on business. She knew nothing else about Mr. Dockins. At least I was counting on that. Finally, Ma responded.

Okay. Be home as soon as you can. I will save you some special food. Tell the family I hope he wins.

I felt relief and texted back.

thnx

Then I quickly pushed send.

The relief faded in an instant. What was wrong with me? I couldn't even feel good that I had *at least* told my mother where I was. I was being responsible. Wasn't I? I tried to relax my shoulders. Another headache was on the verge of hitting me. What would my parents really say to me if they knew what I was doing? Telling them half-truths was their fault, really. Wasn't it? If they would just let me do my thing and not give me crap about everything, then I could tell them the whole truth.

It didn't help any that Billy's text still bothered me. Why had I not just told him about Blake?

"Penny?" I leaned over to Blake's little sister. I had to get my mind off my parents *and* Billy.

"Yes?" She smiled up at me. She held a red colored pencil in one hand, and a blue one was tucked behind her ear, holding back her blond hair.

"I think I'm ready to color another page with you," I said as I reached for the blue pencil behind her ear.

Penny smiled at me as her hair fell into her face. "Yay! I just started one. It's the jungle." She gave me a playful grin. "But I thought we could color each animal either pink or purple . . . or any color that they're not in real life."

I smiled. "Sounds like fun." I felt my shoulders begin to relax.

Chapter 13

5th Place

The energy in the coliseum grew as we all watched Blake step onto the mat to claim fifth place. I had convinced Ms. Long-Hunt and Penny to move down to the Hancock High section of the bleachers so we could get a better view. Ozzie and Zonta were sitting near Tank, a few rows down. Imani, Summer, and Mary Ann sat in the row behind them, leaning in and talking over Zonta's shoulder. Blake had explained that Tank was still in it to win first place, but the finals would happen later that night. Owen and Chastity were sitting on the other side of Tank. Chastity yawned and tried to lean her head on Owen's shoulder. But as soon as the whistle blew, Owen, Tank, Imani, and Ozzie stood up and started yelling, "Fireman! You got this, Fireman!"

Penny's hand tugged at my arm as she screamed, "WHY ARE THEY CALLING HIM FIREMAN?"

"I'LL TELL YOU LATER!" I pointed at her brother, who was already on the mat with the other guy squished under him, trying to grab

Blake's leg. I smiled as the fireman chant grew louder. He told me that he'd won against Carlos by using some wrestling move known by most as a fireman's carry. Since then, the team had nicknamed him Fireman. I could see from Blake's intensity that the team and school's energy was paying off. I looked over at Ms. Long-Hunt, who had her hand over her mouth. She was watching her son and glancing at the screaming bodies cheering him on. I saw a tear escape, and I quickly looked away. I knew at that moment that it didn't matter if Blake won or lost. I could see that his mother felt it was all worth it.

I had never seen my mother look at me that way. I shoved the thought away as I watched Blake make his final move. He pinned the other guy before the end of the first period. Had he really just won 5th place? It happened so fast that I thought I had missed something. Was it all really over?

Within moments, everyone praised Blake, and Tank bear-hugged him, which Blake was not too happy about. After that, his mother and Penny had a chance to give him the attention that mattered most to him. I couldn't hear what they said, but Ms. Long-Hunt reached up and kissed her son on the cheek, and Penny hugged him. He let them and even reached one arm around his mother, patting her on her back. I couldn't help but stare. He caught me watching them, but I didn't look away. Instead, I moved in closer.

"It was nice meeting you, Emma," Penny said as she reached out her hand again.

This time I didn't take her hand but pulled her into a little hug. "It was nicer meeting you!"

Penny giggled as her mom nodded at me. "See you around?"

I wished they'd ask me if I wanted a ride back to Hancock. It seemed I'd bonded some with them, at least with Penny. I glanced at Blake and then back at Ms. Long-Hunt. "Yes, ma'am. I hope so."

Blake dropped his eyes, and his cheeks turned red. Of course, Penny giggled even more. "That's enough!" Ms. Long-Hunt pulled Penny by the hand. "Let's go." She looked at Blake once more. "See you at home?"

Blake nodded and watched them leave.

"You're not going with them?" I asked.

Blake pointed at Tank, who had climbed back up into the bleachers. "Got to stay for Tank's match."

I grunted as I tilted my head. Would this day never end? I felt my headache begin to creep back. "How're you getting home?"

"With Coach and anyone that came on the school bus," he said, clearly not reading my worry. Had I really thought I would be able to catch a ride back with him? I tilted my head to the other side. I had to figure this out. It was almost seven, so it wasn't too late to find my own way home. Not really. I'd be fine. "You're staying to watch, right?" Blake asked, with a huge smile on his face.

My head throbbed. "I really can't. I mean . . . I want to, but I can't." I smiled weakly. "A family thing tonight."

"Okay. I'll walk you out." He reached out his hand, palm up. His eyes dropped a second before his blue eyes looked back at me.

I smiled as I reached out and took his hand. We walked hand in hand. It was really sweet, but it only lasted a few feet before he was over it and dropped my hand. He looked at me to see how I'd react. I gave him a little smile and said, "It's too hot in here to hold hands. We can hold hands some other time." He took a deep breath and grinned.

As soon as we were halfway up the stadium stairs, I dared to ask, "Blake, why are you able to wrestle when you don't really like people touching you?"

He didn't even take time to think but simply answered, "Because of the rules."

I stopped climbing the steps and faced him. "Okay, what do you mean by that?"

Blake stopped, too, and faced me. "There's always a reason for the wrestling moves or the way people touch you. There is one goal. To be pinned or to get the most points. I don't have to figure anything out. If a person holds me one way, then I know what move I need to do next

53

so the match can be in my favor." He shifted. "But people touching me. It stresses me out. I don't know what they want or mean. It's just too much. I can do it when I need to since I know it's important. But my head is always wondering what I'm not seeing, what I'm missing."

I moved in a little. His crystal blue eyes glanced down at me. "So you aren't sure what I want when I get close to you?"

Blake stepped back and laughed. "You're a little easier than most. Right now, you're teasing me. I'm not stupid."

I shoved his shoulder as we both laughed. A few moments later, he grabbed my hand one more time as he walked me out of the coliseum.

Chapter 14

Slammed

Two hours. That's how long it took me to get home. I picked up my phone a ton of times to text Billy, out of habit. But then I shoved it away. I didn't know what to tell him. *Hey, guess what? Blake held my hand. Okay, it was only a few seconds, but I think he really likes me.* It all sounded so silly, so I decided I wouldn't say anything until school.

My stomach growled as I stepped off Bus 33 at the bus stop down the street from our neighborhood. We lived off 19th Street, which was packed with large and small houses, along with two- or three-story condo buildings. A few neighborhoods shot off 19th Street, and I lived in one of those. Ten houses sat along Grove Loop, with only one way in and out. I often wondered about the name since there were not really any trees, and the houses were so close to each other. We all knew each other's business, even if we pretended that we didn't. Still, my parents felt it was a step up from living in the apartment above the fabric store. I did too. One day they'd buy a house along Bence Avenue, with all the classic old homes. Giant oak trees lined the avenue and put on a show in the fall. I suspected that with every new big account they landed, they felt they were a little closer to their dream.

Even though the snow flurries that morning hadn't lasted very long, the cold wind had. I zipped up my jacket and let my hood settle over my head as I walked as quickly as possible down 19th Street. Suddenly, I heard footsteps steps. I couldn't quite tell if they were headed toward me or not, but I didn't want to look up. It was cold enough without giving the wind a chance to blow into my face and freeze me even more. Then, without warning, someone slammed into me. Cursing, I hit the ground hard, struggling to look up. My hands ached from hitting the frozen concrete. I had to force myself to yank my hood off my head, so I could see.

In shock, I sat on the cold ground and looked over at the body that slammed into me. It was also on the ground. But it was wrapped in a huge blanket and was not moving. The string of curse words that came from the blanket told me someone was inside. Sounded like a girl. Then, there were also scratched-up black combat boots that stuck out one end of the rolled-up blanket. I slowly stood up and walked over. The boots moved as the bottom part of the blanket began to curl in on itself. Whoever was inside was pulling the blanket completely over her head. The blanket was wrapped so tightly that it made me think she hadn't had much of her head sticking out in the first place. Clearly, we both hadn't really been able to see where we were going. "Are you okay?" I asked.

"Go away!" The girl yelled with her head still covered. I knew the voice from somewhere, but I wasn't sure who it was.

I felt my cheeks warm. "Hey! YOU knocked ME over. I don't know what your issue is, but—"

"GO AWAY!" The girl's voice was stronger.

I looked down the street. Several cars and trucks were moving quickly up and down Central Avenue, but no one was turning onto 19th Street. I pulled out my phone and stated, "I'm going to call 911."

The bundle shifted. "Why?"

"Because . . . you're hurt. Right?" I asked.

"No, I'm fine. Are you hurt?"

I looked at my scraped palms. "Not really."

"Good. So just go away." The person shifted again before she added, "Please."

I looked at the bundle. It was so weird. Maybe the weirdest thing I'd ever seen. "Are you sure you don't need some help?"

"I'm sure." The voice was still strong. I knew that voice, but I still couldn't figure out whose voice it was, so I started to walk toward the bundle to find out. Whoever was inside pulled the blanket tighter around her head. "What are you doing?"

"Don't you want help getting up?" I stood over her now, but I couldn't see her face or the top of her head at all. "Aren't you going to let me see you?"

"No!"

"Why?" I started to reach down.

"I don't . . . I don't . . . like how I look right now." She said as a matter of fact. "Bad day. Okay?"

I nodded, even though she couldn't see me. My stomach growled, and I pulled my hood back up over my head. It was too cold, and I was too hungry. This bundle of a girl could clearly take care of herself. "Okay. Whatever. You're just a moth hurling yourself toward some big ugly fire. But what do I know? It's your life. Not mine!" I turned and left.

I didn't wait to see what else she would say as I continued walking down 19th Street. She'd been rude anyways, so why should I care? A drop of guilt hit me hard enough to make me stop right before I stepped onto Grove Loop. Was I really going to leave some strange girl, wrapped in a blanket on the sidewalk . . . in the freezing cold? No, I wasn't. I sighed and turned to face her.

But she was already gone.

Chapter 15

First Period

I slung my small neon-yellow duffle bag over my shoulder as I walked into first period, U.S. History. I always switched to this bag during school days, leaving my glossy purple backpack purse at home. Ma fussed at me for not getting a normal school backpack to carry my things. *"Emma, you're not thinking! It will be better for your back and shoulders."* But I refused, of course. Not because I had to have that neon-yellow tote, but because it was NOT what Ma wanted me to have. I pushed Ma's words out of my head as I shifted the bag. My shoulder was sore, but I would never tell her!

"Hi, Emma." Blake stood next to the door. I could see he'd been waiting for me since he'd already dropped off his stuff at his desk.

"Hey." I smiled as he reached over and grabbed my bag off my shoulder. I let him. "Thanks." He slung it over his shoulder as he walked me to my seat. I wasn't sure what to say, so I talked about something

I knew mattered to Blake. "Happy for Tank!" Blake had texted me late Saturday telling me that Tank had won first place in his weight class. Part of me wished I'd stayed, especially since I ate alone that night. My parents had headed to bed early, and Joseph was in his room, studying. So I had curled up on my bed with some of my favorite foods, turned on the TV, and binge-watched an old series. Still, I felt like I had rushed home for no reason. My family didn't even care I was there. "Sorry, I missed it."

"Me too." Blake smiled. "It was really awesome! Once Tank flung the guy to the mat, it was practically over. He spread his whole body weight over the guy and held him down for the pin." He shook his head, impressed. "It's like a whole different way of wrestling . . . you know . . . with the heavyweights." He looked at me. I clearly did *not* know, and from the look on his face, he realized it too. He dropped his eyes. "Sorry."

"Don't be sorry. It's all new to me, but it's still fun to listen to you talk about it." I meant it. I liked being able to see a side of Blake that I had never noticed before. It was fun to see what was going on inside his head.

"Really?" Blake smiled as we reached my desk.

"Really." I reached out and took my bag off his shoulder. "Thanks. My shoulder needed a break."

He smiled again. "Sure." And then he laughed at me as I tossed the bag on the floor next to my desk.

"Are you going to stand there all day?" Lilly Orem, a new white girl to Hancock High that year, was leaning against a desk on the other side of Blake, who was blocking the aisle. What was her problem?

Chapter 16

Lilly

Lilly had her camo backpack slung over her shoulder and was wearing her blue sweater. I was getting tired of that sweater. She needed to switch it up more often. Sometimes the nasty blond hair was clean and pulled back; other times, it was greasy and needed washing. At that minute, it was somewhere in between. I didn't know her well, except for some reason, she was friends with Ozzie and Zonta. Those friendships happened sometime after she came in one morning, and her pale skin was all bruised up. I guessed something bad had happened, but she seemed to have moved on pretty quickly. But to be real, none of that mattered to me. Even though she sat behind me in U.S. History, we pretty much kept to ourselves.

Lilly shifted and asked Blake one more time, "Well, are you going to move or not?"

Blake looked at her and moved sideways. "Sorry, Lilly."

"No biggie." Lilly moved around us to her desk.

I frowned as I watched her plop down into her seat. "You could have walked around." I stated the obvious. Then I felt my anger rise, so I let loose. "There's more than one way to get to your seat! Or do you need a special map drawn just for you?" I wasn't happy with how she pushed Blake around. Why was she talking to Blake in the first place?

Lilly looked up at me and then at Blake, then back at me. She threw her hands up in the air and rolled her way-too-green eyes. "Soorrrryyy. Didn't know it was such a big deal."

I felt heat rise to my cheeks. "You're the one who—"

"It's not a big deal." Blake jumped in. He reached out and touched my shoulder, but for only a second. "I'm fine, Emma. Aren't you?"

I looked at Blake's hand that had reached out and touched me. My anger toward Lilly melted. He was right. I was fine. "Yeah. I'm good." I glanced at Lilly, but she was already opening up her laptop. Why did I have to lose it so quickly? I was proud that people knew I wasn't a pushover. It was who I was to others . . . the girl-with-attitude. I was okay with that. But I was *never* the mean girl. At least, I didn't think so. I really hadn't meant to get so ticked off at Lilly. I took a deep breath, thankful she didn't really seem to care.

"Okay, class, find your seats!" Ms. Williams was already headed to the whiteboard to write something. "We've got a lot to cover today."

Blake turned to leave, so I touched his hand for a second to get him to look at me one more time. He did. I whispered, "See you at lunch." He smiled and nodded but then quickly headed to his seat. I guessed he didn't want to upset Ms. Williams *ever* again.

He'd made some racist statements at the beginning of the year, and Ms. Williams had torn into him. In fact, we were all really pissed at him. But I learned pretty quickly that Blake hadn't quite understood that the things he was saying were hurtful and not funny. He'd only ever heard them from his no-good friends. Once Ms. Williams set him straight, he realized he'd messed up. Then at football practice, he'd had a beating from some of the same guys who taught him the racist insults. Something changed in Blake after that. That was around the time I started to pay more attention to him.

I watched Blake take his seat and then glanced around the room. Ozzie was at the front, near the door as always, with his Cleveland Browns cap on his desk. Then there was Zonta, who was at the very front of my row, gazing out the window. I looked out the window too to see what was so interesting. Nothing much except that the apartment complex being built nearby was making some progress. My attention was pulled to the front of the class, where a few students came in late. Mateo Meza-Moya, a stocky Hispanic boy with his black hair pulled back in a long ponytail, handed Ms. Williams a note of sorts. I never really talked to Mateo, even though he was in my second-period Biology class and my last period, Chorus. He wore white earbuds anytime it was allowed. I never saw him in the hall without them. At that moment, though, he looked ticked. He was never late. Suddenly, I realized something was different.

I turned around and, looking over the top of her laptop, faced Lilly, who was staring at Mateo too. She shifted her eyes to face me. "What?"

I smirked. "I just realized you made it to class on time. Big step for you!"

Lilly cocked her head sideways. "Are you still mad at me for asking your boyfriend to move out of the way?"

Boyfriend. She had said "boyfriend." I couldn't help but smile. "Nope. It's all good." Lilly let out a deep breath as I turned around. I realized she had managed to change the subject. She was something else! I reached down to pull a pen out of my neon-yellow bag that I had tossed on the floor. As I leaned over, I saw Lilly's boots. They were black, lace-up combat-like leather boots. And scuffed up. I sat up quickly and faced her again.

"What?" she asked. This time she just sounded tired. She was so over me. I got it.

"Did I bump into you Saturday night on 19th street?" I asked.

It was a moment before she answered, "I don't know what you're talking about." She fixed her eyes on mine.

"You know . . . with the blanket and all . . . falling down . . . telling me to go away?" I tried to push her.

Lilly pretended to think about it but just shook her head slowly. "Sounds a little crazy. Nope, wasn't me!" Then she looked to the front of the class and stared at Ms. Williams, who was still dealing with late students.

I looked at the side of Lilly's face for a few seconds longer and realized she had just shut me down. She was done talking about it. I shook my head. "Whatever." I turned around and left her alone. It was her business, so why should I care?

Chapter 17

Happy

"The team wants me to sit with them. Are you good with that?" Blake asked as he stood in front of me with his lunch tray. Billy had just sat down across from me, but no one else had joined us yet. I hadn't had a chance to talk to Billy yet about the whole stupid me-not-texting thing.

"Of course. Why wouldn't I be good with that?" I smiled up at Blake. His blond hair was combed back neatly, and his shirt was the perfect fit. He knew how to dress, for sure. Except, after meeting his mother, I guessed she had something to do with it. "You can always sit somewhere else. You don't have to ask me."

He'd been sitting with us every lunch for two weeks. Before that, he had always eaten lunch with his football or wrestling team. Mostly the same jocks. Then after Carlos assaulted Zonta, Blake's so-called friends shut him out. Except Ozzie. The rest had believed Carlos' lies, even after Carlos had been kicked out of school. Blake had pulled him off Zonta before he got very far. But Carlos had twisted the story to turn Blake into a perverted creep who wanted him to attack Zonta. It didn't take too long for the truth to spread. But then, Blake had beat Carlos in a wrestling match at Hemby High. I couldn't believe any school would enroll Carlos after what he'd done to Zonta. But I heard they had because Carlos got off easy since it was his first offense. After that, Blake's team was behind him again. In the last several weeks, Blake's world had been flipped in all sorts of directions. From my point of view, it looked like he had landed with his head held high.

Blake's eyes dropped to his tray and then back to me. "Because . . . you know . . . Saturday and all . . . and first period today?"

I guessed he wasn't just asking me about sitting with the team. He was also checking to make sure I still felt the same way I did Saturday, or even that morning when I told him I'd see him at lunch. I reached up and touched his hand on the side of his tray. He didn't flinch away. "Nothing has changed."

Blake grinned. "Great." Then he turned and left. I watched him as he reached the table with all the jocks. They all cheered as he joined them, and I could see Tank say something that made the whole table laugh.

I thought back to everything he had been through, and at that moment, I was happy for Blake. I was still smiling as I turned back around to take a bite of my apple. I looked at Billy, who wasn't smiling. The intense stare with tight lips only meant one thing. He was pissed.

Chapter 18

Billy

"What're you doing?" Billy stared at me from across the table. His curly brown hair was almost in his eyes. I had told him that letting his wild curls grow to his shoulders would make him look like an out-of-control-poodle. The hair falling into his eyes only proved my point. But the look in his eyes told me it wasn't the time to point it out to him. Not yet.

"What?" My smile began to fade. "I'm eating my apple."

"Stop it." Billy nodded his head in Blake's direction. "What are you doing with *him*."

I let a sly smile form as I asked, "Jealous?"

Billy kicked me under the table. "You know better than that!"

"Ouch! That hurt!" I frowned as I rubbed my shin. Why wasn't Billy up for me teasing him about his gay-self having a crush on me? It had worked before. Why not at that moment? "What's your problem? I just haven't gotten a chance to tell you that Blake and I are sort of seeing each other since Saturday." I looked away as I felt my cheeks warm.

Billy spoke every word like he was spitting them in my face. "You text me every other second." He held up his hand. "Wait! You USED TO text me every other second. How is it you have NOT had a chance to tell me?"

I looked back up at him and swallowed. To be real, I had no idea. Billy was my best friend, so why would I not tell him? Why had I stopped texting him? But since I didn't have an answer for Billy, I played the same game I had started. I lifted my apple up like I was looking for the next best spot to take a bite. "I don't know what the big deal is. So I like Blake and he likes me."

"Do you?" Billy's chin jutted out. "Since when do you *really* like him?"

"Come on, Billy. What's wrong?" I put my apple down into my lunch bag. "You've never had an issue with me crushing on someone."

"This is not crushing. THIS is starting a *fake* relationship. And you didn't text me because you *knew* I'd call you out on it!"

"Whoa. Wait a minute." I glanced for a second over my shoulder at Blake and then back at Billy, whose eyes were staring right at me. I felt heat rise. I was not going to be angry with Billy. I was *not* going to lose it. Not at that minute. I gave him a real smile instead. "Look, Billy, I didn't text you because I was focusing on him." It was halfway true. That counted, right? But I needed him to believe me. My smile widened. "I think I really like him. It's not fake. But calling it a relationship is a little intense." I hadn't told him yet that Lilly had called Blake my boyfriend. I wasn't going to. "We just said we like each other. That's all. It's not like we snuck away into some locker room like Chastity and Owen."

Billy shot his hand in the air. "Stop! Just stop! First of all, ew! I don't need that image. And the locker room? Really? Nasty!" He shook off the thought. As he jerked his head, even his brown curls seemed to shake. "But Blake? You better be really sure you like him before you lead him on anymore."

Suddenly, the anger broke through. My look turned into a glare. "How *dare* you think I'm leading him on!"

Billy lifted one hand to shove his curls out of his eyes so he could return my look. A least a full minute passed with us glaring at each other before he spoke again. "You still haven't answered my question."

"What question?"

"When did you start liking him?" Billy picked up his soda and took a sip. "Was it before or after you knew he had autism?"

"Before!" I spat out as fast as I could and didn't even try to hide my anger. "Why are you such an ass right now?"

72

Billy narrowed his eyes and took another sip. He knew he was pushing me, but he didn't stop. "Are you sure?"

I'd had enough. "YES," I almost yelled. But then I lowered my voice and spat back at him, "You think you know everyth—"

"Chill out and think about it! Will you?" Billy put his soda down and softened his look. "Just think."

I took a deep breath to help calm me down and reminded myself that Billy *was* my best friend. I was the one who had kept something from him. He had a bigger reason to be pissed at me. So I thought for a second. When I felt calmer, I finally answered, "Yes. I started liking him when he helped us at the store, maybe even a little before when his friends started being mean to him. But that was *before* he told us."

"But you already knew before that, didn't you?" Billy's words began to make my head throb. When I didn't say anything, he added, "You told me once at lunch, over a month ago, that you thought Blake might have autism."

"So?" I snapped back. There it was again. I shook my head, more at myself than him. Why was talking about this so hard?

Billy crushed his now-empty soda can. "So I don't want you to do to him what you did to me."

My mouth dropped. There it was. "What're you talking about, Billy? Just say it, will you?" I knew what it was even though we had never talked about it. I thought maybe he'd forgotten. I braced myself. Would this be the end of our friendship? The throb in my head grew. I reached up and pressed a hand against my temple.

Billy looked down at his tray for a second before he looked back up at me and jutted out his chin again. "You only became friends with me when I came out in middle school. Not before." Hearing him say it hurt. Just like I thought it would, which was why I never wanted to talk about it before. I pushed away that part of me that wanted to cry. I didn't cry! I wouldn't cry. But still, I had no words. Billy didn't take his eyes off me as he waited for me to respond.

The pounding in my head grew. I needed to say something, so I tried. "I . . . I . . ."

"Wait." Billy held up a hand. "Let me be clear, I never came out to my parents because they already knew. So I pretty much just came out to my peers. The *point is* that you hoped it would piss off your mom if you had a gay best friend. So you worked really hard at being friends with me."

He was right. I had. I could still see myself so proud that I even told him exactly what I was doing. It had been four years since I had claimed him as my best friend. But if he knew all this, why didn't he chew me out before? Why hadn't he cut me off? I had to know. "So why did you stay my friend?"

74

Billy shoved the empty soda can around on the table between us for a few minutes before he sighed. His chin relaxed as he smiled just a little. "Well, I didn't have many options, did I? I was the first one to come out at our school, and most of my friends stayed away. But not you! You were like a bad haircut that wouldn't grow out. But after a while, you grew on me."

A wave of relief gushed over me. I laughed, but I knew it sounded more fake than real. So I quickly said, "I really *was* crazy!"

Billy reached his hand across the table and grabbed my arm. "Trust me, you still are!" We both smiled. He squeezed my arm as he added, "Just make sure Blake isn't someone else you want to use to piss off your family." Before he let go of my arm, he added, "And don't you dare stop texting me again! You know I've got to know everything! AND you know you need me."

I smiled and nodded. Billy was trying to be nice, and I knew he meant every word. But I could never hurt Blake. And even though I had hurt Billy, that was middle school. This was high school. There was no way I was the same person. No way.

Chapter 19

Rumor

After lunch, I headed down the hall for my third-period class. Blake and I shared first *and* third periods, and I had been looking forward to talking to him in class. At least until Billy had ruined it all. I didn't want to believe Billy, but he'd been my friend longer than anyone, and he knew me better than anyone. Even better than my own family. Still, I didn't want him to be right. I really did like Blake. Didn't I? Of course I did. And I had promised Billy I wouldn't do the same thing to Blake that I had done to him. And the fact was, Blake and I were just getting to know each other. I had plenty of time to break it off if I didn't *really* like him.

All of a sudden, Chastity's arm bumped into mine as she tried to get my attention. She walked next to me like we were close friends, but that lasted all of three seconds. "Heard you and Blake hooked up."

"What? No!" I stopped walking. "Where did you hear that?" The throb in my head that had started at lunch suddenly came back.

Chastity grinned. Her makeup across her cheeks made her look like someone had taken a red crayon to a whiteboard. She came in close. A wavy brown strand of her long hair touched my face. "Don't worry. Just heard it in my own head." Then she giggled. "Got you, didn't I?"

I didn't even know what to say as I stared at the one girl that I didn't want to have anything to do with in the school. Well, let's be real; there were a few others, like Zonta. Still, I didn't know why Chastity kept getting into my business. I took a deep breath. "Don't *get me* like that again." I shook my head. "That's an awful rumor. Please don't start it!" I began to move on down the hall, faster than before.

Chastity kept up with me. "Come on. It's funny." When I didn't answer she added. "I did see you hold hands on Saturday."

I started to get really pissed. I stopped again and looked at her. "Really? All of ten seconds. Yes, big deal!" I pointed down the hall in the opposite direction from where I was headed. "Why don't you go find some real gossip."

Chastity's eyes went wide. "You want real gossip? Because I—"

"No! Stop it. And stop following me." I turned and kept walking.

"Really? It's about your brother." The sing-song tone of her voice made me want to scream.

77

I turned back around and went right up to her. I placed my hand on my hip. "I'm sure it's as good as the lie you just told me."

When I didn't move away again, Chastity knew she had me. Her light green eyes narrowed. "Well, I heard this from my cousin, who works at Good Vibes."

I swallowed. That was where Joseph tutored Zonta. I took a deep breath. I didn't want to know more, but I couldn't help it. "Go on."

Chastity grinned and moved in close. "Well, my cousin told me that she was clearing some dishes next to them and overheard them talking about finding a more private place to study. And then Zonta leaned into your brother and kissed him."

"On the cheek?" I asked. She had me hooked. I didn't want to be, but I couldn't help it.

"Nope. Right smack on the lips." Chastity held my intense stare. She had what she wanted. My full attention. "Like a long-hard-kiss that wouldn't have stopped if he hadn't pulled away."

"I knew she was bad news!" I shook my head. I had just seen Zonta at the coliseum with Ozzie, and suddenly I find out she's making out with my brother. Clearly, he wasn't as into her if he pulled away.

Chastity smiled. "Okay. Well, gotta go!" I frowned at her smile. Was she really that excited to have dropped this news on me? Her smile softened into a concerned look as she touched my shoulder gently.

78

"You can always talk with me if you ever need to, you know?" Then, her big smile returned. "Bye!" She turned, lifted her long curly waves over her shoulders, and left.

I stood in the hall, staring at nothing. I didn't even see the other students as they headed to their classes. All I could see were Joseph and Zonta. Hadn't Joseph learned to stay away from trashy girls? Girls like Silvia? Girls that will only use him? Silvia Hemby was this beautiful bi-racial girl who acted all innocent. But after what she had done to Joseph, I wanted to tear the crown off her head last fall when she was made Homecoming Queen.

Had it already been two years? I was only fourteen at the time. I could still hear my parent's voices. At first, I had wondered why my parents were fussing at my *perfect* brother. I was even a little excited that he was in trouble for a change. I had to hear why. But when I got closer, I heard what they were fussing about. Joseph was telling them that Silvia had been sexually assaulting him as he tried to tutor her. I was in shock. But then I grew angry as I heard my parents tell my brother that if he told people, nobody would believe him. They had also told him it would be bad for the business if he said anything. They had told him to stay quiet.

None of them knew that I was listening from the top of the stairs. I heard every word. I hurt for him. I was angry. Whatever was happening was not right. But Joseph was smart. He found his own way to get Silvia off him. Literally. He said he'd meet her at the library, but she wasn't up for that. Only when she was done with him did Joseph begin to smile again. But he never asked my parents to help him with a problem again. But what problems did he really have? Except, after two years, he was jumping into it all over again with Zonta. Didn't he know better? It didn't make any sense.

Chapter 20

Mad

It took me a minute to pull my thoughts together as I walked into third period. I didn't understand why Chastity was trying to talk to me. She had never really given me much notice until we went to the coliseum together by accident. Still, she could have ignored me that day. I wished she had. But my head really throbbed when I pictured Zonta hitting on my brother. I ignored everyone spilling into the classroom as I stood still. They had to move around me as I dug into my neon-yellow bag for my headache pills and bottle of water. Once I swallowed my pill, I found Blake in his seat, frowning at me.

Normally, Blake and I sat at different sides of the room, but I decided to plop myself down in the empty seat behind him. "Are you okay?" Blake turned in his seat to face me.

"Sure. Why?" I rubbed my temple.

Before he could answer, Zonta suddenly stood in front of him. "Hi, Blake." She smiled sweetly. I felt my anger simmer. How dare she flirt with Blake! Then she looked at me for a second. "Hi, Emma." I glared at her, which caused her sweet smile to slip away. She frowned. "Are you okay?"

"I'M FINE!" It came out louder than I meant it to, but I didn't feel bad about it. After all, it *was* Zonta.

Zonta threw her hands in the air. "Okay. Okay. Sorry I asked." She turned away from me to face Blake. "Soooooo, Blake, I just wanted to say Saturday was so great. Congrats again on your 5th-place win!"

Blake smiled up at Zonta, who was standing closer to Blake than I liked. "Thanks for coming to watch." He looked away awkwardly, like he always did. "And thanks for bringing your friends." He pointed over at Mary Ann, who was waving at him from her seat across the room. She and Zonta sat next to each other and had become closer friends lately. The chitchat lasted a few more seconds before Zonta finally crossed the room to her seat.

Blake faced me again and watched my fingers as they moved slowly in a circle right above my eye. "Are you mad at me?"

I frowned. "No. I'm fine. Really."

"I don't think so. I may suck at reading people, but even I can read you right now." Blake pointed to the front of the room. "You came in here frowning." Then his hand swung toward Zonta. "You yelled at Zonta." Then his hand moved again to point at my hands, still rubbing my temple. "And you obviously have a headache, which you seem to get when you're uptight about something." He dropped his hand, and his blue eyes looked into mine for a long moment before he glanced away. "Are you sure you aren't mad at me for sitting with my team?"

Like a light switch, my anger flipped off. I stopped thinking about Zonta. I stopped thinking about Chastity. And Billy's words were like a faint memory. I didn't quite get what it was about Blake, but at that moment, I started laughing. He looked at me and frowned. I reached over and grabbed his hand. He didn't even flinch. "One thing is for sure. I am NOT mad at you."

Blake's frown melted away, and he grinned. "For real?"

"For real." I leaned forward. It was the closest I had ever been to Blake. He didn't move away, but his eyes darted back and forth from my eyes to my lips. He was trying to read me. He knew I wanted to kiss him, but he was just making sure. As much as I did want to kiss him, I knew others in the class might be paying attention to us. So I hated to back off, but I did, just a little. It would make him think he read me wrong, but I would make it up to him. When the time was right.

Blake began to frown. "So, you're *not* mad?" Blake asked.

I laughed again. "Oh no, I am *very* mad!" Although, at that moment, I didn't feel so mad. "But just not with you."

Blake frowned a little more as he continued to go between my lips and my eyes. "Then who?"

I let go of Blake's hand as I leaned back in the chair. Blake looked a little relieved, but he didn't move as he waited for my answer. I had to think. I shook my head and finally said, "I guess pretty much most everybody else."

This time Blake laughed. He thought I was joking, which I was, in part. It took a second for me to laugh with him because the reality was, I was angry. I was pissed at my parents for expecting too much from me, pissed at Zonta for hitting on Joseph, and pissed at Joseph for letting her. I was also pissed at Chastity's games and pissed at Billy for telling me I was just using Blake. How dare he!

But all that anger seemed less intense as I sat there looking at Blake.

I suddenly closed the gap between Blake and me and kissed him on the lips. It was only long enough to feel his warm lips on mine. But it was long enough to make Blake's eyes shoot open in shock. Then his crystal blue eyes stared at me, not looking away. I tilted my head. I guess it had been the right time, after all.

The throbbing in my temple was pretty much gone. I smiled at him, hoping I hadn't scared him away. It took a moment, but he did smile back. Then, with one swift move, he turned to face the teacher who was calling the class to order.

Chapter 21

Joseph

"Joe, are you up?" I shoved Joseph's half-open door all the way open. My brother was at his desk with his laptop open. I had an idea about how to point out that he needed to stay away from Zonta.

He stopped typing and looked over at me. "Hey. What's up?" He half smiled. I could tell he was tired. "Just finishing off an essay. Due by midnight tonight."

"Oh. Sorry, I'll talk to you later." I started to pull his door closed but took my time so he knew I really needed to talk.

"Wait!" he said. "I'm almost done. Just one last read-through." He turned in his chair to face me. "I still have two hours, so I'm fine. What's up?"

"Nothing," I lied as I stepped into his room again. My plan was working. I had his attention.

"You've got to learn to be a better liar." Joseph laughed. It had been a long time since I'd heard him laugh or even talk to me, since we did our own things, pretty much.

I closed his door from the inside and leaned against it. "I'm failing Biology." I swallowed. If I could get him to feel sorry for me and talk about tutoring, it would be a legit way to talk about Zonta. But at that moment, I realized I hadn't told anyone how I was doing in my classes. I hadn't wanted to face the facts, but if I didn't start turning my grades around in that class, it would be another Emma Tang-Lee failure.

Joseph didn't jump up, run to me, and pull his little sister in his arms. Not his style. Not my parents' style either. "Are you studying?" Typical answer. But one I expected.

I rolled my eyes and added a little whine. "Yes! I just have a hard time getting it."

"I haven't seen you studying." Joseph sounded more and more like my mother every day.

I felt my cheeks warm. I told myself I was in control, but I couldn't help defend myself. "You haven't been here every day after school to see me study." To be real, I sucked at studying. My parents thought they'd drilled good study habits into me, like my brother. But by the time I hit third grade, Tang-Lee Fabrics was taking off. My parents were so busy that they stopped checking and pushing me. So I stopped trying. But Joseph never let up. I always thought he was smarter than me. Yet, I knew deep down that maybe his constant studying had something to do with why he did so well, but he didn't need to know that. And it wasn't why I was talking to him in the first place.

"What's that supposed to mean?" Joseph's voice was much calmer than mine.

I crossed my arms and stared at him. I finally had a chance to say what I wanted to say. The problem was that the anger that had been on mute since I kissed Blake came back in a flash. "Looks like you're too busy after school helping Zonta to care about helping me."

Suddenly, Joseph's eyes grew wide. I had him. "What? What does Zonta have anything to do with you failing Biology?"

"Seems like you're spending a whole lot of time with Zonta. Are you sure it's only a tutoring session?" I had begun to glare at him. "Or has she been able to do what Sylvia Hemby couldn't?" I said it. We had never spoken about Sylvia. We'd never spoken about how he had to find his own way out of her unwanted sexual advances. We'd never spoken about how my parents made him stay quiet. He didn't even know that I knew.

Joseph scrunched up his face like he'd licked a lemon. He always did that when he was disgusted. "How did you know—never mind. You are so amiss right now. What's your problem? Zonta hasn't done anything to you for you to act like she's some back-stabbing wench."

I rolled my eyes at my brother, who liked to use words no one used anymore. "So, Joe, when you say *wench*, do you mean it in the sense of *girl* or *slut*?"

Joseph stood up. I thought he was going to come at me, but he had never hit me before. We never punched each other as kids, either, so I guessed he wasn't going to start at that minute. But his fists curled up as he paced his room. "Don't you ever talk about Zonta like that again. You don't know her, and until you do, you better keep your foul opinions to yourself."

I swallowed. I hadn't seen him this upset in a long time. I realized I may have pushed him too hard. One thing I was sure of, though. He *was* doing more than tutoring. I put my fingers to my head as I tried to make sense of it all. I suddenly realized that I had to tell him one more thing. "But she hooked up with Ozzie right before they broke up. Doesn't that mean anything?"

Joseph stopped pacing and stared at me in shock. At first, I thought he was shocked by the news. But as he stepped closer to me, I saw his anger grow. Toward me. "Get your facts straight! They *never* hooked up. It was a sick rumor. A RUMOR!" He shook his head at me as my mouth dropped open.

"I didn't know." I looked down at my feet. I felt stupid about believing the rumor. I had just told Chastity to NOT start a rumor about Blake and me. But it had been so easy to believe the rumor about Ozzie and Zonta. Still, there was something about Zonta I didn't trust. What if Joseph really liked her? I suddenly felt my stomach turn. She better be real about liking him back! I forced myself to soften my voice. "I'm sorry." I meant it. But not because I thought I was wrong about Zonta being trashy. I was sorry that I had upset him.

Joseph moved back to his seat, trying to calm down. He took a deep breath and looked at me. "Zonta needs my help."

I pointed at myself. "*I* need your help." I had said the words so fast that I was shocked at myself. Did I really want his help? If he helped me, he'd know how much of a joke I really was. He would tell my parents, and then any freedoms that I still had would be taken away.

Joseph stared at me and shook his head. "You've never asked."

I looked down at the carpet. He was right. I never had. I didn't know what else to say. I wasn't going to ask him at that moment because I wasn't ready for his help. All I had wanted to do when I came to his door was to warn him about Zonta and tell him she was probably leading him on. But after all I had said, I was afraid he had stopped listening to me.

I was right. He just shook his head, turned around, and stared at his laptop. He was done with me.

Chapter 22

Rules

I hated myself for even bothering to talk to Joseph. What had I expected? A loving brother who would listen to my concerns? Then there was the fact that he didn't really care that I was struggling with Biology. It wasn't why I had gone in to talk to him. But I had to face the fact that I had just opened the door and let in the thief. I had to be real with myself. Biology was a huge problem. I told myself I would figure it out one way or another, but I was starting to wonder if I even had a clue. I could only pretend for so long that everything would work out.

It was late by the time I headed to bed. I had just climbed under my covers when I felt my phone vibrate.

hey r yt

Blake's text made me smile. Of course I was there. I let my worries drift away as I texted him back.

yes what's up?

r u my girlfriend

I stared at the word. *Girlfriend*. He jumped straight to the point. I wasn't sure how to respond.

do u want me 2 b

do u want 2 b

Why were we texting about this? I had never had a long texting conversation with Blake before. Suddenly, I was tired. Why were we texting about something serious? I didn't want to do this over text.

y r we texting abt this

i can't sleep thinking abt the kiss

I smiled. I could still feel his warm lips against mine.

me 2 so lets talk tomorrow

i need 2 know something now

I raised my eyebrows. What was that all about?

k what

rules

rules?

if u really like someone how do u show it

lots of ways

like hand holding and kissing?

I shook my head. He sounded like a little kid. He couldn't be that out of touch!

sure

so a rule would b if people kiss they are more than friends its not a rule

but is it true

I paused. He wasn't out of touch. He was calling me out.

yes unless one person doesn't mean it

did u mean it today

I paused again. I felt my heart race. He had me. I did mean it. Didn't I? Billy's words made me doubt myself. But I had meant the kiss. I had.

yes

so ur my girlfriend

I smiled.

i guess i am

ok ttyl, girlfriend

I laughed out loud as I pictured Blake grinning. I tapped my phone, ready to text Billy. He'd think it was funny too. But suddenly, my smile faded as I thought of Billy's last words to me. What would he say? Even worse, what would he think? Was I leading Blake on? I didn't think so. I tried to think of the best way to text Billy the news, but I shut off my phone instead. I'd tell him later.

Chapter 23

Just Like That

It was the strangest thing. Just like that, Blake was my boyfriend. We didn't even talk about it again. He sat next to me at lunch. He held my hand when he could stand to and not when he wasn't up for it. Once in a while, we'd steal a kiss from each other. And that was it. Billy didn't say a word. I hadn't told him or texted him because I thought it was obvious, and I didn't need to tell him. At least, that was what I told myself.

Billy still sat with us, as always, and we discussed the latest gossip, like always. Sometimes I'd catch Billy looking back and forth between Blake and me. He was trying to see if we were for real or not. At first, I thought he would get it. See that it wasn't a game to me. It wasn't long before I saw that Billy had his mind set. He wouldn't even laugh at anything that had always been funny before. More times than not, he would look down at his phone. The only reminder that he was still there was when he'd shove his brown curls out of his eyes. To make things worse, Billy seemed to leave the table before us or after us. But what bothered me the most was that he stopped texting me all the time. I told myself that he was just being overdramatic. I hoped he'd snap out of his stupid mood soon.

Two weeks passed, and it was the same thing every day. I became used to the new pattern and enjoyed Blake a whole lot. But that was it. We never tried to get together outside of school. It was like we were a school-couple. It was who we were, but only as we walked the halls of Hancock High. When I realized this was my new reality, I found myself okay with it. I told myself that it gave us a chance to grow as a couple. And it would prove to Billy that I wasn't rushing Blake home just to piss off my mother.

I also told myself that it gave me time to pull up my biology grades. But I made sure my door was closed at home when I was studying. I didn't want Joseph to see me and take the credit for me doing better. But I didn't know why I bothered closing my door because he was hardly ever home. Between going to Hemby University and spending more and more time with Zonta, I doubted he even cared.

I didn't want to face the fact that Zonta had been avoiding me at school too. Let's be real, it wasn't like she talked to me before. But she used to *at least* say hi or smile at me. I just knew Joseph had told her what I had said, because she pretended that I didn't exist. I hated that! It's not like I missed *her* so much, but she was friends with Ozzie. It felt like he had stopped saying hi to me as well.

At least Imani, Mary Ann, and Summer continued to sit with us at lunch once in a while. But I knew they were there because of Billy and Blake. Still, it made me think I could live with my new reality.

Soon March rolled around, and the cold weather gave way to milder days. I kept telling myself that everything would work itself out. I didn't want to face the fact that I was slipping into a deeper hole.

Chapter 24

Missed

It was Friday night, and I needed to get out of the house. I missed hanging out with Billy. In fact, it had been almost two weeks since he had texted me. It was time he got over me dating Blake. Billy was my best friend, so he had to talk to me sometime. I pulled out my phone.

wyd?

It took almost five minutes before he answered.

nothing

I quickly texted back.

can i come over?

tbh no

My stomach dropped. Why was he pushing me away?

u busy?

no

sick?

no

I wanted to cry, but I told myself this was nothing to cry over. Still, I wondered why he was doing this to me. We'd been friends so long. Was he really going to shove me away because he thought I was using Blake? Had I missed something? Did he really think I was such an awful person?

k nvm

He didn't even respond. I swallowed, but I wouldn't cry, even if he was being a jerk. I wouldn't give him that power! But still, I worried. Had I really just lost my best friend? I told myself that Billy would get over it soon. He had to!

Chapter 25

Ready?

"Everyone is very quiet." My father's Mandarin was softer than my mother's. We were sitting at the dining room table for another *special dinner*. Joseph had landed a sweet internship for next summer in Newport. Even though it didn't start for another four months, he'd been informed on Friday. *"You'd think we were at a funeral."*

My brother smiled. *"No, Ba. We're all tired."* Joseph's Mandarin was better than mine. I hadn't spoken it as often as he had. I understood everything, but my refusal to speak it had cost me. My mouth didn't want to form the sounds. I was ashamed to even try. Another Tang-Lee failure. Joseph lifted his chopsticks up, full of noodles. *"I'm honored you've made my favorite, Ma."*

My mother smiled. She was proud. *"Ba and I have spoken with your Auntie in Newport, and she said you can live with her for the summer."* It seemed we had an Auntie or Uncle everywhere, although I had met very few of them. They chatted on and on and on about summer plans all centered around this great honor. I let the Mandarin fade into the background as I focused on eating.

"Are you ready, Emma?" Ba asked.

I knew he was only trying to pull me back into their chitchat. I answered in English. "Ready for what?"

Ba pointed toward the huge wall calendar that they kept next to the door that led to the kitchen. One I never, *ever* looked at since it was mostly full of their business odds and ends. *"Your SAT test. It's in two weeks."* Ba smiled as he took a bite of food.

I almost choked on the noodles that were in my mouth. "What? I already took the ACT in December." Even though I hadn't studied for it, I was happy with my score. To be real, the score was a little below average, but I was thankful it wasn't way-below average. But my parents weren't pleased. I was really getting tired of not pleasing them. I'd even pointed out that the SAT and ACT weren't *really* needed at a ton of colleges. They were beginning to move away from old-school thinking. But the fact was that my parents were very old-school.

My mother jumped in. *"We signed you up in January, remember?"*

I placed my chopsticks next to my plate. I thought I was going to be sick. I suddenly did remember. It had been the same day Zonta had been attacked by Carlos. I had seen the police walk Carlos down the hall in cuffs. So I pushed myself into the girls' bathroom to see what had happened. I took in as many details as possible. I was shocked to see Blake leaning against the bathroom wall with blood running down his arm. Zonta was staring at all of us as we tried to get a look. She seemed pretty shocked. I didn't have much of a reaction to Zonta. She looked like she'd been in a fight, but that was it. Blake, though, looked like he'd won whatever fight had taken place. There was a calm about Blake that made me think he wasn't the creep I thought he was. That whole day I gathered as much gossip as I could. My mind was so obsessed with figuring out what Blake had done that I hadn't paid much attention to anything else. I had just nodded at my mother that night when she told me she'd signed me up for the SAT. I hadn't thought about it since.

"Emma?" Ba poked me with the end of his chopstick. I didn't respond. He switched to English as he poked me a second time. "Hello?"

I pulled out of my daze. "Yes, Ba . . . I'm ready." I lied.

I looked across the table at Joseph. His eyes opened wide. I remembered his words from two weeks ago. *You have to learn to be a better liar.* I hadn't learned. They all knew I was screwed.

Chapter 26

Oak Park

I had to get out of the house! I didn't say anything as I stood up and took my plate to the kitchen. It still had food on it, but I couldn't eat one more bite. No one asked me if I was okay as I grabbed a headache pill and chugged down a glass of water. No one told me to sit back down as I walked past my family, who were all still sitting at the table. No one told me to stop as I grabbed my jacket and walked out the front door.

Even though the night air was chilly, I left my jacket unzipped. It wasn't the same biting cold from a few weeks earlier. I could see inside the houses of my neighbors as I walked along Grove Loop. Most homes were lit up from the inside by their T.V.s. A few shades were drawn on second levels, and one home was pitch dark. How many people were looking into our home? How many people looked through our dining room window, all lit up with bright lights? How many people wondered what was wrong with me? I needed to get out of there!

I picked up my pace and turned right onto 19th Street. Then I took a left onto Oak Road. I was headed to the only place I knew where I could be alone. Oak Park. It was a playground complex off 17th Street and Oak Road, only a few blocks away. A wooden pirate ship had been built. Slides spilled down each end. The masts had wooden ladders that stretched up to small platforms. From there, rope ladders dropped to the ground. It was the newest and most exciting place to be when I was a kid. My parents even let me ride my bike to the park on my own. I would hurry there after school and play for hours with anyone who was willing to let me join their games. I missed those days.

As I walked closer to the giant pirate ship in the dark, it felt strange. A new chain-link fence wrapped around the park, leaving only one entrance. A large sign read *Closed from Dusk to Dawn*. My childhood playground was off-limits, but I didn't really care. There was nothing for me in the shadows of the dark ship. I sighed and started moving along the fence. It felt good to let my fingers touch the cold metal. Suddenly, I saw someone walking toward me down the path I had just come. I stood still until the person came closer and slowed down.

"Oh, it's you." Lilly's face came into view as she walked under the same streetlight where I was standing. Her green camo backpack was pulled over both shoulders. A colorful fuzzy blanket was shoved through its top loop. In one hand she was carrying a Hancock Burger bag, and in the other, she held her jacket. She had on a green T-shirt with bold yellow letters that read *Having a good time at Food-Time Grocery?*

"What're you doing?" I asked. I guessed she lived somewhere nearby, but I didn't really know where. Lilly frowned at my question and ignored me. It took me a second to realize that it came off as rude. So I pointed at her shirt and added. "I mean, are you just getting off work?"

Lilly nodded. "Yep." Then she walked past me and headed for the gate to the playground and walked right into the darkness beyond the fence. I stood there with my mouth wide open. What was Lilly thinking? She wasn't allowed in there!

Chapter 27

Dusk to Dawn

"Wait! Lilly." I ran up to the open gate to Oak Park and stopped. "You can't be in there." When she didn't respond, I decided she hadn't heard me. I had to go in and tell her. So I looked up and down the street first and saw no one coming before I headed to the spot where I had seen Lilly disappear. It wasn't really so dark once my eyes adjusted. The streetlights flooded the perimeter of the park, leaving enough light to see a bit. "Lilly?" I called out a little louder. "LILLY?"

"Will you shut up?" Lilly was suddenly standing in front of me without all the things she had been carrying.

"You're not supposed to be in here." I almost whispered.

Lilly dropped her shoulders. "No, Emma, *you're* not supposed to be in here."

I didn't want anyone to hear us, so I walked a little closer to her. "That doesn't make sense. The sign says—"

"*Closed dusk to dawn*. I can read." She pointed at me. "So you need to go now."

I shook my head. "Why me and not you?"

Lilly sighed, clearly tired. "Look, Emma, it's closed for people who want to play or come here and do whatever you people do . . ."

"You people?" I spat back at her. She was asking for a fight. I had enough anger that it wouldn't take much for me to start screaming at her. Or anybody, really.

Lilly rolled her eyes. "Sorry. Let me be specific." She softened her voice. "You *rich* people."

"I'm not rich," I argued, but the fight was not there. Compared to her and her nasty camo backpack, I guessed I looked rich. Suddenly, I wondered why her backpack was missing. My eyes grew wide. "Where's your stuff?"

Lilly didn't answer. Instead, she climbed up some wooden steps and jumped onto the ship's platform. Then her head ducked down and she was gone. But I knew exactly where she went. I shook my head as I climbed the steps. Just as I remembered, in the middle of the ship, there was one opening that had wooden steps that led you into the belly of the ship. I turned on the flashlight on my phone and headed down the steps. There was still one large space with several low-to-the-floor wooden benches, but it wasn't as large as I remembered. My head almost hit the wooden boards above me, and the benches were no more than a foot high. Just as I suspected, Lilly was in the far corner on one of the low benches. With her legs stretched out in front of her, she sat on her blanket and opened her Hancock Burger bag. She had a flashlight propped up so the beam hit the ceiling, enough light to create a small, well-lit area. "Look, Emma, I'm hungry. Been a long day. I don't really have energy for this right now." She pulled out her burger and took a huge bite.

I turned off the light on my phone and sat down on the low wooden bench across from her. We weren't very far apart. I stretched out my legs so my feet rested near her backpack. "Are you . . . are you . . . going to sleep here?"

Lilly swallowed, pulled a soda bottle out of the side pocket of her backpack, and took a sip. "I haven't decided yet."

"So you do sleep here sometimes?" I asked. I felt a chill, so I finally zipped up my jacket. Lilly must have felt it too since she grabbed her blue sweater out of her backpack and pulled it on. Then she shoved her jacket on as well.

"Sometimes. But just *dusk to dawn*." She suddenly looked up at me. Her way-too green-eyes searched mine. "I live at the corner of 19th and Maple. It's not like I don't have a place to go."

"Then why come here?" I didn't understand.

"Sometimes I just need my space." She looked away and bit into her burger again. I didn't know much about Lilly. But one thing for sure was that she sucked at lying too!

Chapter 28

Point of View

Memories of playing in the belly of the pirate ship as a child hit me as I watched Lilly finish her burger and fries. Never would I have thought that one day I would be sneaking in after dark to find someone eating their dinner in secret. It seemed, maybe, that Lilly was full of secrets.

It didn't take long for her to finish her burger. When she had chugged down the rest of her soda, she burped really loud. I couldn't help but giggle.

"Well?" Lilly looked at me as she shoved the bottle into her empty Hancock Burger bag. "Why are you still here?"

I looked toward the steps. There was nothing else to look at, but I didn't know what to say to Lilly. I'd been so focused on her story that I had pushed away why I was there in the first place. I wondered what I should tell her. I settled on the truth. "Not ready to go yet. I guess." To be real, it was the truth, but a lot of missing facts. My specialty.

"Oh, yeah . . . totally get it." Lilly's sarcastic tone made me face her. She threw up her arms. "Seriously? That tells me nothing."

My cheeks warmed. Who was she to give me crap? I pointed at all her stuff and spat back at her. "Oh, and you're telling me a whole lot too!"

Lilly raised her eyebrows. "True." She pulled the blanket up, wrapped herself in it, and then leaned over to rest her head on her backpack. She stretched out her feet along the bench. She barely fit. Clearly, she had decided to sleep in the belly of the ship after all. As soon as she settled, she said, "Stay or go. I don't care."

Even though Lilly was trying to dismiss me like everyone else, I noticed one thing. She didn't turn off her flashlight. She wasn't going to leave me in the dark. Not yet. I couldn't go home yet. Nothing had changed. I couldn't keep pretending everything would be okay. I had to talk about it. I had to get it out of me, or I would burst. Suddenly, I had an idea. I didn't know Lilly and she didn't know me. She just told me she didn't care, but maybe that was what I needed. Maybe I just needed to talk with someone who really wouldn't care about me. There would be nothing she would expect from me. But I could at least get it all out. I took a deep breath. "Okay, so I'm screwed." I waited a second. When she didn't say anything, I asked. "Lilly? Are you still awake?"

"Yeah. You're talking, aren't you?"

"True." I scooted down to lie on my own bench. I needed to see her face to see she was listening. The flashlight was the only thing between us. She just stared at me like she didn't care how close I was. This was good. Listening, but nothing more. "I'm never good enough. I can't get good grades, and I'm always letting my parents down. If I can't figure out how to bring up my grades, then I won't have a chance at getting into a good school, and I may not get into a school at all. I'm sure my parents already think I'll end up in some dead-end job." Lilly blinked, but there was no smart-ass response. She was still listening. "Tonight, I found out that I have to take the SAT in two weeks, and I'm not ready. Are you ready?"

Lilly's eyes grew really wide. "I'm sorry, but—" She broke out into the loudest laugh I had ever heard come from her. I didn't know why she was laughing, but she kept laughing until she had to wipe away tears.

"What's so funny?" I asked, holding back since I really wanted to scream at her. She was only a couple of feet away, and I had opened up to her. I had expected her not to care about what I said, but not to laugh at me! I took a deep breath.

Lilly finally stopped laughing and looked at me again. "Emma, what do you think? Do you really think SAT and ACT scores even matter to me?" I looked at her face. I had never noticed the circles under her eyes. Her dirty-blond hair was starting to be greasy. When I didn't answer, she added, "Look, we all got our stuff. For me, I just have to take it a day-at-a time. Seems like you got to figure it out a whole lifetime-at-a-time. Looks like it sucks for each of us where we are."

I saw Lilly for the first time. Her life was nothing like mine. And yet, she didn't tell me her life was worse. I smiled just a little. "Maybe there's somewhere in between a day and a lifetime?"

Lilly yawned and smiled back. "Maybe. If you figure it out, tell me." Her eyes closed, and she fell asleep. Just like that!

I lay next to Lilly for another twenty minutes or so. I watched her eyes and her breathing as she slipped into a deep sleep. She trusted that she would sleep through the night. Safely. In the belly of that wooden pirate ship. I couldn't imagine how that could feel safer than home. But at that moment, I trusted that Lilly knew what she was doing. I turned on the light on my phone before I turned off Lilly's flashlight. Then I climbed the steps onto the ship's main platform, slid down a cold slide, and headed home.

Chapter 29

Lights Out

As I walked along Oak Road, something shifted. I had felt better for a moment. Lilly had been right. I didn't have to figure out my whole life that night. One test or one grade was not going to doom me. My list of failures didn't have to define me and who I would be one day. But as I moved closer to 19th street and further away from the park, a darkness began to hit me.

Lilly was still at Oak Park. Alone. She seemed so sure about sleeping in that playground. I stopped walking, turned around, and looked down the road. Should bring Lilly home with me? But she seemed okay. She made it look like she was just camping out, like she could head home if she wanted to. If I woke her up, she'd probably be pissed.

Then there was my family. I had stormed out of the house and did not let them know where I was going. I hadn't even checked to see if they had texted me, so I pulled out my phone and looked. Only Joseph had texted. A bunch of times.

You okay?

Ma and Ba are worried but won't text you. Don't want to push you further away. Call me if you need me to come get you.

Emma? Hello?

Guess you're too good to text back.

Don't do anything stupid!

I shoved my phone back into my pocket. What would they think if I brought a stranger home? Would that be *doing something stupid*? I turned back around and headed home. Lilly would be okay. She believed it, so I needed to believe it too. I couldn't have one more strike against me with my family. Not that night.

Almost all the lights were out in my house as I walked up to it. I could see they'd left the hall light on for me and my parents' light was still on in their bedroom, although the shades were drawn tight.

I locked the door behind me and headed up the stairs. When I walked past my parents' room, there was no light spilling out from under their bedroom door. I sighed. I always told myself that they didn't care, but they had clearly been worrying. As soon as I was home, they could finally sleep. How many times had they done that? How many times had I not noticed?

I lifted my hand to knock on their door, but Ba's snoring stopped me. What I had to say could wait for later.

Chapter 30

First Period

For the first time ever, I waited for Lilly to walk into U.S. History. I hoped she was okay.

"Hi, Emma." Blake came up next to me and squeezed my hand, but then let go.

I smiled up at him. He was wearing a new T-shirt. At least it looked new to me. Spring couldn't arrive fast enough. We were all ready to ditch our heavy jackets. "Hey, Blake. Did you have a good weekend?" I asked, not really paying much attention to his response. I kept looking at the classroom door. Zonta walked in and caught me staring in that direction but quickly looked away. Ozzie and Mateo and most of the class had already arrived. What was I worried about? Lilly was usually late.

"Are you listening?" Blake asked.

I looked up at him again. "Sorry. No." I didn't bother pretending with Blake. He could handle facts and seemed to like that he didn't have to read between the lines with me. "What did you say?"

He explained how he'd worked later hours at Food Time Grocery that weekend. "Even Lilly stayed late." Suddenly he had my attention.

"Really? So, Lilly doesn't usually work that late?" I asked.

Blake thought a second. "Well, actually, she works as many hours as she can get. But Stew doesn't always hand out the extra hours to her." Blake took a deep breath. "But I think he should since—" Blake's eyes grew bigger as he caught himself.

"Since what?" I thought back to a few weeks ago when Blake was chill with Lilly asking him if he was going to stand in her way or move. He was not upset at all. It was like they knew each other, but I didn't realize until that moment how well they knew each other. They worked together. But Blake never talked about Lilly. Ever!

Blake took two deep breaths and looked everywhere except at me. "Nothing."

I frowned and tried to take his hand and squeeze it. "What aren't you telling me?"

Blake pulled away from my hand. "I promised her I wouldn't say anything." He took one more deep breath before his crystal blue eyes stared right into mine. "So, don't ask me to."

I had learned how important rules and routines were to Blake. I wanted to push him, but I didn't want to push him away. If I asked him to break a promise, then I was going to lose that one thing between us that I really liked. I got him, and he seemed to get me. It was hard to explain. I smiled at him and reached up and kissed his cheek. "I won't."

He nodded, clearly relieved. His eyes suddenly grew wide. "But you can always ask her."

I laughed. "Trust me, I will."

"Okay, class, let's get started." Ms. Williams drew our attention to her. Blake quickly moved to his seat behind Mateo. Mateo slowly pulled out his earbuds and opened his laptop, as did the rest of the class. Except me. Where was Lilly?

Chapter 31

All Good

Halfway through class, Lilly walked through the door. A few people glanced up, but most people were used to it. Even Ozzie and Zonta barely paid attention to their friend. Lilly walked right up to Ms. Williams with a note. Lilly's hair was wet, and she was not wearing the work shirt that she fell asleep in the night before. Ms. Williams handed Lilly her laptop before Lilly headed to her seat, lugging her camo backpack. She'd pulled her blue sweater through the top loop. I wondered where she'd stashed her blanket.

She plopped down in her seat behind me, and I turned to face her. "Are you okay?"

Lilly's eyes went wide, and she put on her best smile. "Yeah, I'm all good." She opened the laptop.

"Why does Ms. Williams keep your laptop for you?" I whispered.

Lilly peeked over her laptop at me. "Why do you think?" She disappeared behind her screen.

Emma

I sighed and felt stupid for even asking. If she was sleeping in the belly of a wooden pirate ship, then a laptop was the last thing she needed. Still, I wasn't finished. "Why is your hair all wet? Did you go home this morning? Is that why you're late?" I hoped the answer was yes, so I wouldn't feel as badly for leaving her alone the night before.

Lilly poked her eyes over the top of her screen again. "I showered here." Then she disappeared again.

I frowned, leaned my head to the side of her screen, and whispered. "Why're you just telling me little bits and pieces? And what is it that you told Blake that he can't tell me?" I couldn't wrap my head around her life. Around her world.

"Miss Tang-Lee? Is there a problem?" Ms. Williams walked toward us. I sat up straight.

As soon as she came close enough, I answered her. "No problem here."

As Ms. Williams looked at Lilly, her eyes softened. "Everything okay?"

Lilly smiled. "Yeah. Just like I told Emma, I'm all good."

As Ms. Williams headed down our row to help a student who held his hand up, I leaned to the side of Lilly's laptop one more time. I whispered as quietly as I could, "I'm not done with you yet!"

Lilly was trying not to laugh as she answered, "That's for sure!"

Chapter 32

Biology

I didn't have time to corner Lilly after class, but I would some time. I just wasn't sure when that would be. At that moment, though, I had other worries. To be real, I had thought a lot about what Lilly had said in the belly of the pirate ship. I didn't have to figure out my whole life all at once. I had more choices than I thought I did. So I made a plan. A plan to shorten my list of failures. I had to find a way to pull up my biology grades. I figured if I could get my grades up, then maybe my parents would be okay with me *not* taking the SAT test. The test I wasn't ready for, at all.

"Excuse me?" A white girl from my biology class, with her hair dyed pink, walked up to me before class started. It was second period, and I was sitting next to Mateo. We had been sitting at the back of the classroom, next to each other, the whole semester. But we rarely spoke. Not because we didn't like each other. Because we really didn't care. At least I didn't, and from what I could tell, neither did he. At times, I wondered if we sat next to each other to begin with because we knew that we would leave each other alone. It had worked. Until that Monday morning.

"What, Tammy?" I looked at the girl who was holding her notebook. I could see her neatly written notes. She was one of those girls who made sure she had the teacher's attention and was always asking questions. She sat at the front and had her own collection of friends. That's all I really knew about her. Except that she had never walked to the back of the classroom to talk to me.

"Can you help me understand the different kinds of cell transport?" She held out her notebook and pointed out a list of words to me. Tammy smiled and added, "I just don't really get how they all work, and I missed last Friday."

I frowned. "Why are you asking me? Ask your friends."

Tammy leaned in and smiled awkwardly. "Well, I don't really want to because they aren't always right." She stood up straight, and her smile faded. "I need to get it right!"

I looked over at Mateo, who shifted in his seat. He had already taken out his earbuds but wouldn't look at me or Tammy. I looked back at the pink-haired girl, still frowning. "So why are you talking to me if you want to get it right?"

121

Tammy looked at me, confused. "Well, you're Asian. Aren't you?" My eyebrows shot up. I didn't know what to say. Tammy felt like she needed to explain. "I mean, the Asians are the smartest people, right? I mean, most of them are in the advanced classes, but we at least have you." I looked at my classmates; we were a combo of races. But she was right. Most of the Asians *were* in advanced classes, along with other non-Asian teens, which didn't seem to matter to Tammy at all.

I didn't have the energy to point out to Tammy that not all Asians were in advanced classes. AND there were only about thirty Asian students at Hancock High. There were others in the community too, but several went to a private school in Newport. It wasn't just Tammy. What most of my classmates didn't understand was that it wasn't that Asians were smarter because they were Asian. It was the intense pressure to achieve. It was a whole other level of pushing us from an early age. A pushing that my parents gave up on with me when their business became their focus. Still, I had the same pressure on me . . . that expectation that we would do more and go further than our parents. It was knowing the sacrifice they had made so we didn't have to struggle. We owed them. So we worked hard. To be real, everyone worked hard except me. But I didn't need Tammy pointing it out.

"Look, Tammy." I reached out my hand and slapped Mateo's arm. "Ask Mateo. He's the smartest one in here." Which he was.

Mateo swung his head around. His dark eyes narrowed. "Don't slap me!" His black hair was back in a ponytail, and the fuzz on his face looked like he was trying to grow a beard. "What?" Mateo looked between Tammy and me.

I pointed at Tammy. "I know you heard her. Racist Tammy here needs help with cell transport."

"I'm not racist." Tammy was shocked by my statement.

I raised my eyebrows. Even though I was simmering, I remained calm. "You just said Asians are the smartest people."

Tammy swallowed. "But that's a good thing." She really believed her blanket statement about one race was a *good* thing. "I didn't say anything bad."

I shook my head. She was too much. "Look, whatever. Let Mateo help you."

Tammy looked at Mateo. His stocky size and intense stare didn't help my case. But he didn't say no. He waited for Tammy to say something. She looked between Mateo and me a few times before she finally said. "It's okay. I'll just ask my friends."

As she turned to leave, I couldn't help myself. I yelled after her. "Is it because he's Hispanic? Are all Hispanics scary? Does that mean you can't trust that he'll help you?"

123

Tammy glanced back and frowned at me but didn't say anything as she tucked herself back into her seat and huddled up with her friends.

Chapter 33

Mateo

"Thanks a lot!" Mateo glared at me.

"What?" I tilted my head and pouted. "Did I hurt your feelings?" Mateo looked away, so I slapped his arm again, but softer. "Come on. You know I'm speaking the truth."

Mateo shook his head as he turned to face me. "I told you not to slap me."

I lifted both hands in the air. "Sorry. That was more of a tap, don't you think?"

Mateo stared at me for a second. "Look. You do you. But I don't want to have *anything* to do with you being mad at the world."

I frowned. "I'm not mad at the world." Was this guy for real? I was trying to get him to lighten up, but he was turning the whole thing around. Making it my problem, when it clearly was not!

Mateo raised his eyebrows. "Right."

I wasn't going to let him place the blame on me, so I pointed at the three girls huddled over Tammy's notes. "Look. You know Tammy was being racist."

"Or falling for deep-rooted stereotypes," Mateo said, still staring right at me.

"Same thing." I couldn't believe he was taking Tammy's side. I couldn't believe I even cared. I should have never brought him into it in the first place!

"Not true." He argued.

Trying to stay calm, I folded my arms and lifted my chin. I wanted Mateo on my side. Maybe I could still play this out in my favor. "Okay. Teach me oh-wise-one."

Mateo looked around the classroom. Everyone was talking or working, waiting for the teacher to stop explaining something at her desk to two boys who were arguing some point with her. Clearly, he had time. He rolled his eyes and looked at me again. "It's complex."

"I can do complex." My chin was still up, but I gave him a sly smirk. It was a challenge to stay with me if he dared.

"Okay." He was willing to play my game, but I didn't let my body show the relief I felt. Instead, I looked right at him as he explained, "So if she were *really* being racist toward you, she would have tried to put you down in some way because of your race. Make you feel less than her. Or, let's say . . . she told you that you can't take this class because you're Asian." Suddenly, he glared at me. "Then there's outright prejudice statements. Like if she had said that all Asians are scary, so you can't trust them."

"Oh." I swallowed and dropped my chin. Had I really said those very words about Hispanics? No wonder he was trying to blow me off. "Sorry about that. I guess I took it too far."

Mateo shook his head. "You think?" Mateo took a deep breath. "Look, we all throw out stereotypes all the time. Or at least think them."

"Still not right," I said softly. I had thrown out that awful statement and felt like a real idiot. I had done what I accused Tammy of doing. Whatever challenge had been in me a few seconds earlier had disappeared. All that was left was the real me. "Mateo, I'm sorry I said that . . . I don't really—"

"Doesn't matter." Mateo stopped me. "Once it's out, it's out." I swallowed as I kept eye contact with him. My throat tightened, but I kept myself from crying. Not happening in front of Mateo! As he watched me hold myself together, he slowly started to smile. "Trust me, I've heard worse."

127

I sucked in a quick breath. He was giving me a chance to pull myself together. It worked. I shook my head and swallowed before I could finally respond. "Doesn't make it right."

He nodded. "Never does. But, after a while, you build your walls and figure out how to protect yourself."

I dropped my eyes. We all had our walls. When I looked back up, Mateo was looking toward the front of the classroom. The teacher was finally gathering her stuff together to teach. I had a few seconds left so I leaned toward Mateo. "Pssst."

"What?" He rolled his eyes. "Class is starting."

"Do you think you can explain the different kinds of cell transport to me?" I smiled awkwardly.

Mateo searched my face. "For real?"

I nodded. "For real."

Chapter 34

Lunch

"So, how long have you been dating?" Billy asked at the lunch table as he bit into a french fry. He sat in his usual seat across from Blake and me. Imani sat on the other side of Blake with Summer and Mary Ann across from her. Billy had never stopped eating with us, but he hadn't talked directly to me in at least a week. He focused on everyone else and acted like I wasn't there.

But at that moment, instead of me being excited that he was even talking to me, I rolled my eyes. He *knew* how long, but he was just pointing out the fact that I *was* dating Blake. Something he still didn't think was real from the start. I wondered why he was even eating lunch with us since that was the only thing that he really did with me. He didn't text me anymore or respond to the ones that I sent him. But still, I hoped that it meant he wasn't completely done with me.

Something had to give soon. I didn't have a bunch of other friends. There was so much I wanted to talk about with Billy, but I had to keep my mouth shut. He had to want to talk with me first. He had to decide I was still worth it.

"Exactly two weeks today." Blake jumped in and grinned. He wasn't reading Billy like I was. Even Imani frowned a little at Billy as he took a dramatic bite of a second fry.

Imani, ignoring Billy's attitude, elbowed Blake gently. "Sweet!"

Summer made some whistling noise, and Mary Ann just laughed at the over-the-top celebration of our two-week mark. I thought they were overreacting, but Blake ate it up. He was proud.

Billy shoved another fry into his mouth. But it was Summer who smiled and asked, "So, how's it going?"

Billy's eyes moved from me to Blake, clearly waiting for a response. I felt my shoulders tense, but I teased, "None of your business—"

"Great," Blake answered.

Summer and Mary Ann grinned at Blake. I couldn't see Imani's face. But I could tell they were happy for Blake. Imani quickly asked, "Really? What's so great?"

Billy leaned in and shoved his curly bangs out of his eyes. "Yes, *do* tell!" He said dramatically. Blake kept grinning since he wasn't reading Billy's body language. Blake's eyes looked up to the ceiling. I knew he was thinking about what parts he should share.

The girls were too focused on Blake to care about how Billy was acting, but I shot him a look. He just smirked at me and then returned his focus to Blake.

When Blake didn't answer fast enough, Summer jumped in and asked, "So where have you gone together?"

Blake shared, "Mostly first period, lunch, and third period. Sometimes we talk after school when we wait for our busses."

There was a moment when no one spoke. Billy let his eyes move between all of us as he chomped another fry. Waiting. It was Mary Ann who asked what everyone was thinking. "So you haven't really gone out on a date? Or really left the school together?" She wasn't being mean. She was just piecing together the facts. The very strange facts.

Blake frowned and looked down at his own fries. "Well, no."

I'd had enough, so I reached out and squeezed Blake's hand as I looked at Mary Ann. "Does spending lots of time at the state wrestling tournament count?" Then I forced a smile and added, "That is, if anyone is counting."

Imani leaned in so she could see me around Blake. "No one's counting, Emma. We're just having fun."

Summer reached one hand up, pointing at the air. "You mean to say the two of you have never really gone out together?"

Blake answered before I could. "That's right. I guess it's time we do." He smiled at me. "Looks like we needed a little push to take the next step."

I swallowed and smiled. "I guess so."

Summer, Imani, and Mary Ann started laughing. Summer looked right at me, "Let me know if you need any help with what to wear."

I stuck out my tongue. "Very funny."

A few more jabs were thrown before the girls settled into a different conversation. I looked over at Billy, who was staring at me. He shook his head, ate another fry, pulled out his phone and ignored me for the rest of lunch.

Chapter 35

Invite

I hated it that Billy thought it was all a joke. Because it wasn't. I wanted to text him, to tell him it was real. But I didn't. I was over him judging me. If he was really my friend, then he'd start texting me. But he had to do it first!

I pushed thoughts of Billy out of my head as I grabbed Blake's hand. We managed to hold hands almost the whole way from the cafeteria to 3rd period together. As soon as we were close to our classroom, Chastity and Owen came around the corner. He had his arm draped over her shoulders. His red hair looked all mussed up, and her make-up was smeared. She ran her fingers through her brown waves of hair, trying to pull them back into a neat ponytail. Clearly, they had not been at lunch. I pushed away the thought and hoped we could walk past them without talking. We weren't that lucky.

"Hey, you two!" Owen smiled. "If you ever want to know some good places to hide . . . there's a costume closet between the boy's bathroom and the chorus room. It has a broken lock."

"Nope, I think we're good." I quickly answered. I liked being a couple with Blake, but I didn't want to be that kind of couple.

"Hide?" Blake asked. "Why would we want to hide?" Owen and Chastity laughed. So Blake looked right at me. "What're they talking about?"

I could feel my cheeks warm. He asked me a direct question, so I gave him a direct answer. "They go and find a private place to make out during lunch."

"Make out all the way!" Owen leaned into Blake. "If you know what I mean?"

Blake's eyes grew wide, and he let go of my hand. He finally got it.

Chastity's light green eyes suddenly lit up. She leaned up close to Owen and whispered loud enough for us to hear. "You should invite them to your party on Friday night."

Owen smiled wide. "Yeah! Why didn't we think of that before?" He looked at both of us. "Party at my house. Friday! Starts at seven. You don't have to bring—"

"Will Carlos be there?" Blake interrupted.

Owen's smile dropped, and he moved away from Chastity, who whimpered a little. The red-headed jock moved close to Blake. I was proud of Blake for not flinching away. Owen's voice was low but serious. "Man, I promise you, Carlos is out of my life. Haven't seen him since you took him down." Blake just nodded as Owen added, "I wouldn't do that to you. Okay?"

Blake looked at Owen briefly before he dropped his eyes again. "Okay."

Owen's grin returned, and he reached his arm out for Chastity, who quickly snuggled back next to him. "See the two of you Friday?"

Before we could answer, the two lovebirds disappeared into a classroom.

"What was that about?" I asked Blake as I reached for his hand again. He let me.

"Carlos was always at all of Owen's parties. When Carlos spread the lies about me, I stopped being invited." He looked at me. "Just had to be sure before we go."

This time I dropped his hand. "Do you really want to go to that party?"

Blake frowned. "Well, it makes sense." A smile began to grow. "We need to go somewhere, and Owen's house is pretty awesome! You've got to see it. It could be fun."

Billy had been close friends with Owen when they were kids, and Billy had told me the Hemby's home was huge and on Midway Lake. I'd never been to one of the houses along the lake. I was impressed that Blake already knew how great the home was. I sighed and reached for Blake's hand again. "Okay, why not?"

Chapter 36

Chorus

The day always ended with Chorus. The one thing I had in common with Mateo was that we both loved to sing. He really had the best voice out of everyone, but he never boasted. To be real, he never said much in class to anyone except the teacher. But when he sang, we all listened.

I loved chorus class not only because of the singing, but because it was mellow. We did what we needed to do. We practiced more some days than others. Then there were days we could spend the last thirty minutes of class talking or doing homework. I'd usually settle for talking or checking my phone. The teacher didn't really care if we sat inside the classroom or out in the hall. Most everyone stayed in the room, but Mateo always chose to go out in the hall. He'd sit on the floor and lean up against some lockers as he listened to music. It was no different that afternoon.

I scooted into the hall with my neon-yellow bag slung over my shoulder. He was so into his music that he didn't see me standing there looking at him. So I moved in closer and scooted down next to him. Well, not right next to him. My bag was between us, and he had some notebooks in a pile on the floor next to him. He pulled an earbud out of one ear. "What's up?"

"Not much," I answered. "What're you listening to?"

He handed me the earbud, and I pulled it to my ear, forcing us to lean in a little to each other. The music was some rock song I'd never heard before. "Who is it?"

"Shhh. Listen." Mateo was set on me doing more than getting a glimpse into his music. So I shoved the earbud in so I didn't have to hold it. And listened. A guitar solo took me on a long journey before the lyrics even began. They drew me in.

I looked at Mateo, but his eyes were closed, so I closed mine, too, and listened to the rest of the song. Once it was over, I pulled out the earbud and handed it to him.

"Jimmi Hendrix singing *All Along the Watchtower*," Mateo stated but quickly held up his finger to stop me from responding. He added, "I like Hendrix's version the best, but Bob Dylan wrote and recorded it first."

I waited for him to drop his hand before I spoke. "I really liked it."

"Me too." He leaned his head back against the locker.

"Is this what you're always listening to?" I asked.

Mateo turned his head to look at me, but it was still resting against the locker. "Not only Hendrix. All of the rock greats. I love those long-drawn-out pieces with crazy-sick guitar solos. Then there are those lyrics that make you think."

I nodded but didn't say anything. I watched Mateo close his eyes again to keep listening. That's when I saw one of his notebooks was wide open, and I couldn't help but read what he'd written. "What's the truth? Can anybody tell me? I see through your lies. You can't hide from me."

Mateo suddenly opened his eyes and grabbed his notebook out of my hands. "What're you doing?"

"Are those someone's lyrics too?" I asked.

Mateo shoved the notebook into his backpack. "No." He hesitated a second. "They're mine."

"Wow. I can't wait to read the rest of the lines."

"Well, you won't!" He answered quickly as he settled himself back against the locker. "I can't get any further than those two lines."

I leaned my head against the locker too. We sat there quietly for a few min before I said, "I like the line *What's the truth? Can anybody tell me?*"

139

Mateo lifted his head and smiled. "Yeah?" As I nodded, his smile faded. He looked at me like he was trying to decide if he should share his thoughts with me. Then Mateo leaned his head back again and said, "The line that stands out to me right now is *I see through your lies. You can't hide from me.*"

I frowned. "Are you making a point?"

"Do I need to make a point?" Mateo closed his eyes again. When I didn't answer, Mateo asked. "What do you want from me, Emma?"

I felt my shoulders tense. But when I looked up at Mateo's closed eyes, I realized Mateo wasn't challenging me. At least not in a mean way.

I could have blown him off, but I didn't. Maybe it was his closed eyes, or maybe it was his lyrics. For whatever reason, I took a risk and spoke the truth. "I need your help with bringing my grades up in Biology. I'll be lucky if I get a C or a D." When Mateo didn't move, I added, "I think you might be the only person who can help me. I mean, really help me."

Mateo turned his head and looked at me. "Why is that?"

I looked down and crunched up the strap to my bag. "Because we may be more alike than not."

Mateo laughed. I'd never heard him laugh. "Emma, I'll help you. But one thing is for sure, we're not alike *at all*."

I frowned. "Why not?"

Mateo nodded his head toward the opening to the chorus room. "This is the first time you've ever come out into the hall to sit with me. You're angry with the world, but you can't get enough of it at the same time."

I felt my chin begin to stick out. "You look pissed at the world too!"

Mateo looked straight at me. "Don't mistake *quiet* and *careful* for being pissed."

My mouth dropped. I didn't really know Mateo. But I'd very quickly learned that there was more to him. I dropped my eyes and almost whispered, "Will you still help me?"

Mateo leaned his head back on the locker. "Sure."

I smiled. "Great. Give me your phone number." We put our numbers in each other's phones. But as he handed me back my phone, he looked right at me again. "But there's one thing . . . I'll need your help too!"

"With what?" I was surprised. What could Mateo possibly need from me?

Suddenly, students began to pour out into the hall. Class was over. Mateo smiled, "I'll tell you later."

Chapter 37

Stubborn

What did Mateo need me to do? I started to freak out. I threw my bag on the floor and flung myself on my bed. It was only 4:30 in the afternoon. It seemed Monday would never end. I pulled out my phone and found Mateo's number.

k its later

I stared at my phone for five minutes before I realized he wasn't texting me back. I got up and walked across the hall to Joseph's room. The door was closed, but I could hear him laughing. Then I heard a girl giggle, so I knocked on the door. Hard. "Joe? Are you home?" Obviously, he was.

The door flung open, and Joseph stood there still smiling from whatever had happened two seconds earlier. I looked past him and saw Zonta sitting on his bed. Books and note cards were spread out.

In an instant, my anger shot out of me like a flame. "So I guess you did find a more private place to study." I hadn't even tried to stop the words from spilling out of me. The pressure in my head began to build, but there was no way I was heading to my room to grab a headache pill.

"What's that supposed to mean?" Joseph's smile disappeared.

Zonta moved off the bed and walked toward us. She shoved her hands in the back pockets of her jeans. "What's going on? You've been acting really weird lately."

I crossed my arms and leaned against the door frame. My cheeks were warm, and my chin was up. My left temple began to throb, but I didn't let it distract me. I didn't even try to hold back. "So have you! You and Ozzie don't even talk to me anymore."

Zonta's eyes grew wide. "It's hard to! Whenever I try, you glare at me!"

Was she really making it all my fault? I dropped my arms and pointed at my brother. "I know Joe told you what I said, and that's why you stopped talking to me!"

Zonta looked at Joseph. "Told me what?"

Joseph sighed and looked at me. "Really, Emma?" He pointed at all the cards spread across the bed. "I thought you could study for the SATs with Zonta today. She was okay with it. So I invited her over to surprise you."

I felt my throat tighten, and my eyes began to tear up. I had screwed up. Big time. They had come to help me. They were reaching out to me, and I had shut it down before they even had a chance. My headache hit me full force, and I suddenly grabbed my head and closed my eyes. The tears had to stop! When I opened my eyes again, I found Joseph and Zonta staring at me like I was crazy. They couldn't see me cry! No one saw me cry! Ever! But I couldn't stop myself. Not that time.

Suddenly, I started shaking, so I turned, ran into my room, and slammed the door behind me. I swallowed two headache pills before I flung myself onto my bed with my feet dangling off the side closest to the door. And cried. It was the most out-of-control feeling I had ever had. Between sobs, I could hear Zonta and Joseph talk, even though it was mostly a muffled sound. A few words stood out, like *Silvia* and *didn't know*. At one point, Joseph's voice got louder as he said, "It won't do any good. Trust me, she won't listen to you. She's too stubborn!" A second later, I heard a knock on my door.

"Emma?" Zonta waited a moment before she turned the knob and cracked my door. "May I come in?" I didn't answer. Not because I didn't want to answer but because I was afraid that if I opened my mouth, I'd sound like an out-of-control baby. I had to hold onto any self-respect that was left. Which wasn't much. To make things worse, my head was still pounding since the meds still hadn't kicked in yet. I took some

144

deep breaths trying to calm myself down. I heard the door close again, but then I felt my bed sink down near my feet. "Emma? I'm sorry."

I sniffled as I scooted my body around so I could see Zonta. I swallowed and found my voice. "About what? It's not your fault I assumed the worst. Or that I *always* assume the worst." Mateo was right. I was angry at the world. I rolled my eyes and added, "or that I glared at you for no reason. Or that—"

"Okay, stop." Zonta shook her head. "Emma, I'm sorry because I had no idea you were so upset with what happened between Joseph and Silvia."

I stared at Zonta, surprised. I hadn't expected her to go there. Joseph had clearly just filled her in on the details. Yet, she still came in to talk to me. She pulled her thick, curly brown hair to the side and her brown eyes seemed to look right into me. I had never really thought about how pissed I was at Silvia for sexually assaulting my brother. Or how pissed I was at my parents. I felt something well up inside of me again, and I began to shake. "It's not right . . . it's not fair." I sobbed. Then I cried out, "If it had been me, people would have done something." Then my eyes went wide, and I stopped sobbing over my brother's pain. I looked at the hurt in Zonta's eyes. It was the first time I got it. My anger gave way to guilt. How could I not have seen it

145

before? I barely whispered. "Like you." Zonta began to tear up, but she didn't look away. I could barely speak. "Like Carlos did to you."

A few tears escaped, but she didn't look away. She wasn't going to hide anything from me. "That's right."

I reached my hand out and touched her knee, but only for a second. I couldn't remember the last time I reached out to comfort anyone. "I'm sorry . . . I'm sorry I didn't get it before."

Zonta reached up and wiped away her tears. She made a low growling noise. "Ugh. I hate crying."

"YOU hate crying?" I practically laughed. "I NEVER cry, and look at me now, an ugly mess!" Then I looked at her. "Did you just growl?" I felt a sudden lightness. She didn't go on about what an idiot I was or how dare I even have those thoughts about her in the first place.

Zonta shrugged. "I do that sometimes." She gave me a half smile.

I wiped my face with the back of my sleeve and took a deep breath. I wondered what to say next. We sat there for at least a full minute in the quiet. I finally found my voice and leaned into her as I gave her a little shove with my shoulder. "So you like my brother?"

She snorted, shoved me back, and nodded. "That's for sure."

"Because he gets you?" I asked, knowing the answer.

Zonta smiled. "And because I get him. We're helping each other heal."

146

I nodded. "Okay." I took another breath, sat up straight, and flung one hand in the air like I was some queen. "You can date Joe."

Zonta laughed. "I didn't know I needed permission."

I stuck out my chin. "Well, don't tell Joe, but *he* needs my permission. He just doesn't like to admit it." We both giggled. I hadn't giggled in a while. It was a new energy. It was different, and it felt good.

Suddenly, there was a knock on the door. "Everything okay in there?" Joseph sounded worried.

I held my finger to my lips. "Shhhh. Not a word."

Zonta giggled and snorted again before she answered, "Yes, everything's fine."

To be real, everything wasn't fine. But at that moment, that angry part of me had shrunk some. I had pushed my hate for Silvia onto Zonta, which was not fair to Zonta. I saw Joseph and Zonta differently after that. But I still didn't study with them. I was too far behind. Yet, I was grateful they at least tried.

That day, something in me shifted. In a good way. It had been a long time since I was grateful for anything. But it wasn't only that I liked that they had tried to reach out to me. I was also grateful that I didn't need to hate Zonta anymore. I had let that hate go, and I could feel the relief across every inch of my body. Most of all, my head. The ache hadn't just become a dull throb like all the other times. Instead, it was almost completely gone.

I had to really think about who else I was pushing my anger on. Who else was I wrong about?

Chapter 38

Stand Out

I was just about to fall asleep when my phone vibrated. I thought it might be Blake, but it was Mateo.

whats up

its later

and?

u said u'd tell me what u need from me

When Mateo didn't answer right away, I texted my one crazy worry.

its not drugs is it

really? that's not racist at all

I frowned and realized he was right. Why had I even thought that? Had I assumed that he would ask me about selling drugs because he was Hispanic and kept to himself? Or was it because I really thought it might be a logical tradeoff for getting help with grades? Or was I repeating the same mistake that I had just decided I would stop making. I had to stop judging others before I knew what the deal was!

sorry. sux to b me right now. everything i say or think is messed up k

so what is it. jf its not drugs 😜

fabrics

?

i need some help with costumes for a battle of the bands competition in april. my band's tight on cash for some costume-like jackets. we want to stand out. mad cash prize and connections

I laughed out loud. It was the funniest thing that had happened to me that day. Mateo was in a band and wanted material to sew something. My whole body relaxed. I realized it would involve my parents. But when it came to me and grades, there was a good chance they'd help out.

k. let's do this!

rock on!

I rolled my eyes and smiled. Within minutes I was fast asleep.

Chapter 39

First Lesson

"So, when are you going to help me?" I leaned into Mateo as Biology was getting ready to start. Everyone was still headed to their seats or talking with their friends.

Mateo turned his head and grinned like he was going to have fun with whatever he had in mind. "You've got to do what I tell you to do. Agreed?"

I frowned. "What? No way. What if it's creepy or just wrong?"

Mateo's face went blank as he rolled his eyes. "Really? This again?"

I sighed. "Sorry. I did it again."

"Yep!" He shook his head. "You really don't trust anyone, do you?"

I thought for a second. I *did* have people I trusted. Like Billy, even though he didn't want to have anything to do with me at that minute, and Blake and even my parents. Maybe even Joseph and, now, Zonta. But I didn't always believe everyone made the right choices or knew what was best. Or at least not what was best for me. Wasn't that different than trust? But after what had happened with Zonta, I was learning that maybe I did have more people that I could trust. "Not true." I smiled at him. "I just forgot that you're new on my list of people to trust." I held my smile as Mateo thought about it. I decided to offer one more peace offering. "I'll do what you say. I promise."

Mateo nodded and then pointed to the girls at the front of the room. "First lesson. Go ask Tammy if you can have a copy of her notes."

My eyes shot open and mouth dropped. "What? Why?" I had been so rude to Tammy the day before. I tightened my shoulders. It wouldn't be long before the tension traveled to my head.

"Think about it," Mateo explained. "What does Tammy do better than anyone in the class?"

I knew the answer. "Take notes." I leaned into Mateo. "But I thought you took great notes."

"I do, but—" Mateo pulled open his notebook and held it out for me to take a glance.

"It's messy." I frowned.

"Not to me." He closed it. "But you need good notes to study from, and I'm guessing your notes aren't great."

"True." I nodded. I struggled to listen and take notes. It was always the same thing. Once the teacher moved to the next concept, I was not ready to move on. I always missed at least half of what was said. I looked at the girls and then at Mateo. "She'll never share them with me. Not after yesterday."

152

Mateo shook his head. "I bet she will. Just be nice." He snickered. "That's a real thing, you know?"

I glared at him. "Thanks a lot."

"Go on." Mateo waved his hand like I was a child he was trying to move along.

"Okay, okay." I stood up and took a deep breath. I could feel the tension in my shoulders ease. I could do this. This was good practice! I moved slowly toward the girls. Tammy was the first one to see me walk up to them. She shifted awkwardly and looked away. I had been so awful. Before the girls could say anything, I blurted out, "I'm sorry for what I said yesterday." It was hard to say since I was still bothered that she could so easily stereotype all Asians. But I didn't really know Tammy, right? There had to be something more.

Tammy's eyes widened, and a sweet smile appeared. "Emma, that's so kind of you." I didn't know Tammy enough to know if she was being real or just playing me.

I cleared my throat. "I was having a bad day, and I said some things that I shouldn't—"

"Stop right there." Tammy's hand flew up. She shook her head back and forth dramatically. Her pink hair swinging along for effect. "I shouldn't have said those things."

"No, she shouldn't have!" The friend closest to her agreed. It was a brown-haired white girl named Trish. The other friend, Nicole, nodded along as well. I'd forgotten about Nicole. She was bi-racial, part Asian and part African American. I realized Tammy probably got an earful when she told them what had happened.

I smiled at the three of them. They were clearly so proud of Tammy being in the know. Tammy grinned at my response. "Oh, good. You're not still mad at me."

I shook my head. I couldn't believe Tammy was worried about me being mad at her. She regretted her words from the day before more than I did. "No, I'm not." I actually meant it that time. I glanced at Tammy's notebook and remembered why I was there to begin with. "I was wondering if I could copy your notes after school, if that's okay? I'm struggling with getting good notes . . . and . . . well . . . we all know yours are the best."

Tammy's eyes shot open, and her smile widened. "Yes! Of course! I was hoping to find a way to make it up to you. This couldn't be more perfect." She smiled sweetly as she cuddled her notebook. "Like it was meant to be!" I smiled back, thinking she was a little over the top. But it was all in my favor. We talked a few more seconds and planned to meet at the library after school, where I could photocopy her notes. Then I headed back to my seat.

Emma

As I walked toward my desk, the smirk on Mateo's face told me something was up. That had gone way more smoothly than I had expected. As soon as I sat down, I leaned into Mateo one more time. "You overheard them tearing into Tammy yesterday, didn't you?"

Mateo shrugged. "You know, there are a few perks to being invisible to most people."

Chapter 40

Pick Up

I told Blake I could pick him up at his place on Friday and drive us to Owen's party. Ma said I could use her car since she and Ba weren't going out. I'd told them that I was going to a party at the Hemby's home on Lake View Drive. *And* that I'd go there with Mr. Dockins' son. There was a lot of room to read between the lines, so they said yes. I still hadn't told them I was dating Blake. Billy's words had hit me hard, so I still didn't want to bring it up. If I told them and my parents became upset, which they would, then Billy would be right. And I didn't want him to be right.

My parents each had a car, and Joseph had bought himself a used one. I didn't drive much since most of the places I wanted to go were close enough to the bus stops. But to reach Owen's house, I needed some wheels. We didn't want to take two buses and then walk along Lake View Drive for a while. Blake told me he hadn't gotten his license yet, which wasn't a surprise. Seemed like most guys my age weren't driving yet. Half of them told me they could get most places without a car, so what was the point? The other half was too busy gaming to take the time to learn to drive. I didn't really care one way or the other and I didn't mind picking Blake up.

I followed the directions off my phone, but I started to worry when it took me into a part of Hancock I had never been to. It was already dark as I drove along Hill View Drive. Houses and townhomes gave way to larger buildings. At first, I thought some new condos had gone up. But when lawns turned into slabs of concrete, I knew I was wrong. Had I punched in the wrong address? I stopped right in front of some huge buildings with a sign that read Hill View Apartments. Each building looked like it had six floors. Even though I had never been there, I had heard of the place. Did Blake really live in Hancock's public housing?

Streetlights lit up a huge chain-link fence, which wrapped around one side of the closest building. It created a fenced-in courtyard of sorts, which was also lit up by several floodlights. A few teens were shooting some basketballs as a handful of little kids climbed some old monkey bars. I remembered when the monkey bars had been torn down in the small park in the center of Hancock's old town across the street from Tang-Lee fabrics. They weren't safe. A very fancy playground and park were built to upgrade the public face of Hancock. Clearly, that upgrade hadn't reached Hill View Drive.

A few of the people standing around started to stare at me. Then I realized that I had stared at them first. So I quickly looked away. I parked on the side of the road and checked my phone. Had I done this right?

All of a sudden, there was a knock at my window. I jumped so hard that I almost dropped my phone. Penny was looking through my window, trying to get my attention. Her huge smile calmed my nerves so I rolled down my window. "You almost gave me a heart attack." Penny had pulled her blond hair up into high ponytails, with most of her hair still down, almost an exact copy of mine.

"Blake forgot his jacket and is coming right back down." She grinned and whispered, "So you're going on a date?"

"Something like that." I glanced at the towering buildings. "You live around here?" I asked, wondering why this would be their neighborhood. The way the whole family dressed made me think they had a nice house in Bence.

"Yes! That's our building!" Penny pointed to the one behind the monkey bars. Coming out of the shadows, I saw someone wave at me. It took a moment to realize it was Blake walking toward us.

"Aww." Penny fussed. "He's already here." I turned back just in time to see fingers slide through my window and touch my arm. "Did you see my hair?"

"I did!" I patted Penny's hand. "Very nice!"

Blake opened the car door and got in. Before he said anything to me, he spoke to his sister. "Penny, Mom said to go upstairs right now. We'll wait for you to get inside."

Penny sighed. "Okay." She waved at me. "Bye, Emma!" Then she took off and skipped all the way past the monkey bars up to the building. She turned one more time to wave at us before she slipped into the shadows.

I wasn't quite sure what to think or even how to react. I felt the familiar simmer rise. I knew one thing for sure. It was not at all what I had expected.

Chapter 41

Confused

"So you live here," I stated. There had to be a good reason. I didn't need to be pissed. Not yet. I pulled out into the road and made my way back along Hill View Avenue. I knew that if I took it all the way back to 17th Street, then I could follow 17th all the way across town, past Hancock High, and toward the lake. Blake would tell me where to go from there.

"Yes, we do," he answered, but then he didn't say anything else. I felt my cheeks grow warm. Why wasn't he explaining to me that he was poor? Was his total rich-boy image a lie? I glanced over at him and noticed that he was looking out the window. He'd told me once that he liked to count the stop signs. I wondered if he had decided it was a good time to do that. Better than talking to me. But I needed to talk. "So, how long have you lived there?"

"Since I was ten. After my stepdad died." He let his head lean into the window, still looking outside.

In my rearview mirror, I could see the public housing fade out of view. I calmed my simmer and decided to take a different angle. Maybe I was missing something. "Blake, are you okay talking about this?"

For the first time, I could feel him shift his body to look at me. I couldn't look into his eyes, but maybe that was okay. "Not sure why I wouldn't be?" He really didn't think it was a big deal. So if it wasn't a big deal, then why did he hide it from me?

I gripped the steering wheel a little tighter. I didn't want to get angry. I wanted the night to be fun, but I couldn't just let it go. I wasn't sure how to explain what I was thinking. "Well, I mean . . . I thought your family had . . . you know . . . money. The way you all dress . . . you know . . . like you all jumped out of some fashion magazine."

It took a moment, but suddenly Blake started laughing. "I'll have to tell Mom! She'll be really proud!"

I wanted to laugh too, but it wasn't funny to me. I felt like I didn't really know much at all about Blake or his family. Just because Mr. Cole Dockins had money didn't mean Blake did. I should have known that. To be real, who works at Food Time Grocery unless they really need the money? I suddenly realized that Blake and Lilly had *that* in common, and it was probably the secret she wouldn't let Blake share.

I didn't know what else to say. I hated that it was still a big deal to me, so I shut up. I didn't say anything for a good fifteen minutes. We

161

were heading down 17th Street before Blake spoke again. "Is it a problem?"

"What?" I asked.

"That I'm not rich?" Blake asked the same way he might ask if I like my food, or if I thought it was going to rain or not.

I didn't answer him right away. He was so calm, and his question was so real. I was surprised that my anger didn't come raging back. Instead, I had to think. I *was* bothered. But was I bothered because he didn't have money? Or because I didn't know? To be real, I didn't care if his family had money or not. "I don't think so," I responded honestly.

"Okay." Blake leaned his head against the window again. "Good."

As we passed Hancock High, I cleared my throat. I still needed to clear up one more thing. "I mean . . . I'm pretty confused why you didn't tell me you didn't have money and that you lived . . . you know . . . at the Hill View Apartments."

Blake didn't even lift his head off the windowpane. He simply answered, "You never asked."

Chapter 42

Wrong

We didn't talk the rest of the drive except when Blake told me where to turn. I wasn't shutting him out or pissed off about what he said. It wasn't even an awkward silence. It was peaceful. I thought a lot about what he had said and how much Blake made sense. I hadn't asked him about where he lived. I had assumed a whole lot. It wouldn't have been fair to Blake if I had shown him my anger because my anger was based on *nothing* he had done. I felt relief. For once, I had caught myself before I said something I would regret. I wondered if I could learn to do that with other people.

Who else had I been wrong about?

Billy.

But HE had stopped texting me!

Didn't he?

Suddenly I remembered. I was the first one to pull away. It was at the wrestling tournament when I had first shut Billy out. I didn't tell him about my crush on Blake. I had always told Billy about everything.

He had always helped me talk through all my thoughts and feelings. Except, when I worried that he might be right, I shut him out. But he wasn't right. I was just afraid he would be right. I began to shake my head. Was it really not about Blake, but about me pushing him away?

"What's wrong?" Blake's voice broke into my thoughts. "You're shaking our head and making a funny face."

I sighed as I turned on my blinker to make our final turn onto Lake View Drive. "I just realized that I screwed up big time. I've been reading someone wrong for some time now."

Blake laughed. "Welcome to my world!"

Chapter 43

Party

It was almost eight before we pulled up to Owen's house along Midway Lake. The house was three stories high and had a large porch wrapped around the front half of the house with several large white pillars. I needed to stop thinking about how to make things right with Billy. I needed to focus on Blake and get us talking about something. Anything. So I pointed out one odd thing about the old but fancy house. "Who needs three chimneys?"

Blake laughed. "That's exactly what I asked Owen when I first came here." It felt good to hear him laugh.

There weren't many cars, so I parked in the driveway. "Well? What did he say?"

"He had no clue." Blake grinned. "But I looked it up."

Of course, he did! I looked at him. "Well? Tell me."

Blake's grin widened. It wasn't only fun to see him get excited about facts, but he got a kick out of me wanting to hear those random facts.

"It's because it's so old that each room on each floor used to need a fireplace to warm the house."

"So there are more than three fireplaces in that whole house?" I was really listening. It was good to move on from my almost-meltdown over picking him up in an unexpected neighborhood.

"Ten, if I counted right, since the chimneys have more than one flue in them." When I frowned, he explained, "That's the passageway for the smoke to go up the chimney."

"Cool." I smiled at him.

He didn't say anything else and neither of us was in a hurry to jump out of the car. We were peaceful together. I looked at the handful of cars and suddenly felt uneasy. "Are we early or something?"

"No, we're late. But I don't get why there aren't more cars. I've never been to one of Owen's parties without cars parked along the street." He looked over at me. "Should we go in now?"

I nodded but didn't smile. "I guess so."

We both climbed out of the car and up the porch steps. Blake rang the doorbell, but it took a few minutes for anyone to answer the door. Just as I was about to suggest we leave, the door opened. "There you are!" Chastity flung open her arms and embraced me like a long-lost friend. The alcohol smell was strong. "Thought you were never gonna come."

Owen came up behind her, pulled a handful of her long hair to the side, and kissed her neck. For a second, he was hidden behind the wavy brown strands that broke loose. But then he looked up and gazed out at us, clearly a little drunk or high. "Come on in!" As we entered a large, well-lit hallway, we faced a grand winding staircase in front of us. Owen waved to the opening on his left *and* on his right. They were mostly dark, except for the glow coming from the fireplaces. I could barely see into the rooms.

Suddenly, a tall white guy with light brown hair came up to us with his arm slung around a pretty Hispanic girl. "Hey Blake!" The guy smiled, but I couldn't quite remember who he was.

"Hey Gavin." Blake nodded. "What's going on?"

I suddenly recognized Gavin. He was the football team's captain, but he was also one of the guys who had been a jerk to Blake during wrestling. Clearly Blake had moved on, but I still didn't like the guy. Gavin lifted the Hispanic girl's chin and kissed her. She giggled and pulled away. Gavin looked back at us and smiled. "One guess."

Before Blake could respond, Gavin pulled his girl into one of the rooms. So, I took a step closer to get a better look and saw couples were either talking to each other or kissing.

I suddenly felt a little sick and slowly stepped backwards. "I don't think—"

"Pick a room and a couch." Owen wasn't even trying to listen to me. Then he pointed at the stairs. "Unless you don't want anyone watching. There are more rooms upstairs." Chastity giggled. Then she turned around and full-on started making out with Owen. She shoved him to the stairs, and they made it up three steps before he just sat down, and she straddled him. Waves of her brown hair spilled over them like a curtain.

"Kind of hard to get upstairs now," Blake stated. I looked up at him. I wasn't sure if I should laugh or be shocked. Was he teasing? Or was he wanting to take me upstairs? What was this party? His eyes quickly found mine, but he looked away and back at me so often that I knew he was not at ease. "Are you . . . uh . . . are you . . . wanting . . ." He flung out his hand and pointed at the make-out mess in front of us. "That?"

Relief hit me hard. I reached up and gently took Blake's face in my hands so he couldn't look away. "Hell no!" Then I gave him my biggest smile.

The relief in his eyes melted my heart. "Good." He reached up and took my hands from his face but then held them as he still faced me. "Because I'm not ready for . . . you know."

I smiled and soaked up the beauty behind those crystal blue eyes. "Same here. Should we leave?"

Emma

He frowned. "But what about our first date?"

I knew he was trying to prove he could take me on a date, but I realized that he had already proved the most important thing to me. We were a match. I squeezed his hand and pulled him out the door. "I have a better idea."

Chapter 44

6th Street

I drove us back along 17th Street, past Hancock High, and then down Central Avenue. Blake kept asking me where we were going, and I told him he'd have to wait and see. I pulled into Hancock Pizza and bought a large pepperoni to-go. By then, Blake had stopped asking.

I kept driving south along Central Avenue and turned west onto 6th Street. Blake looked around and stated, "We're getting closer to where I live."

"Really?" I said as I pulled into the third house on my left. 6th Street was the best example of what Hancock used to look like in the old days. A time when anyone who was anybody lived within walking distance of the courthouse. As Hancock grew and modern neighborhoods offered more, the old blocks were forgotten. Some homes were handed down to relatives that still lived in the area. Like Billy's family. The first Seabergs to settle helped found the city. Billy's family, Roxy and Will Seaberg, only had two ways to prove that they had any ties to

Hancock "royalty." One was their last name, and the second was the old two-story home. A relic that needed a new paint job.

I'd never been further west along 6th Street, which was why I never knew how close Billy lived to Blake. I guessed we were still around six to eight blocks away. The front porch light turned on as I explained, "We're going to hang out with Billy."

"Does he know that?" Blake asked as Billy opened the door. He wore some p.j. bottoms and a white T-shirt, clearly ready for bed. He gawked at us as I put the car in park.

I smiled. "He does now."

Chapter 45

Roxy

"What are you doing here?" Billy asked as I walked up his porch steps holding the pizza.

"We're having our date night with you." I smiled and hoped there was still a part of Billy that would play along. That part of him that used to be able to tell when I really needed to be with him.

"You could have texted me." Billy fussed.

"So you could tell me no! Or worse, not even respond." I shook my head. "Not a chance."

"Not my fault." Billy shot back. I started to wonder if I had made a mistake dropping in on him. I pushed my fear away, since I really didn't know what else to do to get his attention. I had to at least try.

I looked him right in the eyes and answered, "You're right."

Billy, confused by my answer, looked at Blake. "Is this your idea of a date night?"

Blake shrugged. "Better than Owen's idea." I laughed out loud, which made Blake smile.

Billy frowned. "What?"

Blake thought about it for a second and then began. "Well, when we got to—"

I rolled my eyes. "I don't want to relive it." Then I shoved Billy to move him out of the way. "You can fill Billy in later when I'm not around! Pizza's getting cold." I marched right into his home. The familiar musty smell brought flashbacks of all the movies we had watched over the years on his couch. It had been almost a month since we had watched a movie together.

"Okay. Make yourself at home." Billy said with a bite as I threw the pizza down on the coffee table.

"Emma? Is that you?" Billy's mother came around the corner and gave me a huge hug. "Haven't seen you in a while." She had the same curly brown hair as Billy, but hers was long and neatly pulled back. She was the only older woman I called by her first name. I'd called her Mrs. Seaberg at first, but over the years, she told me that she needed me to call her Roxy. She told me it made her feel closer to me. So I did as she asked, but I just didn't tell my parents. As Roxy stopped hugging me, she eyed Blake up and down. "Well, who is this?"

"Roxy, this is my boyfriend, Blake." I grinned. Billy crossed his arms and just stared.

"Oh, aren't you a cutie." Roxy started to walk straight toward Blake with her arms wide open. Blake began to back up.

I moved toward the over-the-top-loving woman and touched her arm. "Blake has autism and doesn't like to be touched. At least not by complete strangers." Blake relaxed as the woman dropped her arms.

Roxy focused on Blake, trying to figure out what to say. She spoke very slowly. Too slowly. "I . . . am . . . so . . . happy . . . to . . . meet you!"

Blake frowned at Roxy and then looked at me. "What's wrong with her?"

Suddenly, Billy lost it. He laughed so hard I thought he was going to pass out. I was shocked to see him laugh at all, but it was a glimpse of hope. Maybe Billy could snap out of it. Maybe.

Roxy's eyes and mouth shot open as she stared at Blake *and* Billy. I touched her arm again. "Blake is one of the smartest people I know. He has autism, but that doesn't mean he can't have a normal conversation with you. He just might avoid eye contact, or he might be really direct."

Roxy shook her head. "Direct, for sure." Then she smiled. "But I like direct!" Billy finally stopped laughing. It felt good to see him laugh again. Roxy hugged me one more time. "So good to see you. I'm headed to bed. William is already asleep. He'll be sad he missed you."

I glanced over at Billy for a second before I dared to respond. Billy looked at me before he looked away. It looked like he wasn't quite sure what to think. I decided to take a chance, so I smiled at Roxy and said, "I'll be back." I loved the attention Billy's parents gave me.

Roxy headed down the hallway as she added, "You kiddos, have a good time." I hoped Billy would stop being so pissed at me, so I could keep my promise. If he was willing to hear what I had to say, then I knew I might have a chance.

Chapter 46

Good Time

It was awkward at first. I sat on the couch next to Blake while Billy plopped himself down in his dad's recliner. It was as if he suddenly remembered he was supposed to be pissed at me like he hadn't just burst into laughter a few minutes earlier. The T.V. was on with a random movie flashing across the screen. We each grabbed a piece of pizza that was barely warm. I felt a dull throbbing begin at my temple. If I didn't say what I really wanted to say, I would have a full-on headache before the night was over. I swallowed a pill with a huge gulp of the soda that Billy had pulled out of the fridge. I let the caffeine ease the pain a little as I waited for the medicine to kick in. A huge burp escaped, but the boys didn't make some joke or even react at all. It was that tense!

I started to take another bite of pizza but then stopped. "I need to say something." I finally spoke as I put my half-eaten pizza on the edge of the Hancock Pizza box.

Blake grabbed his second piece of pizza and then turned to face me as he took a huge bite. Billy, though, didn't even look at me. He was busy balancing two pieces of pizza on one of the chair's arms. "Billy, I have something to say to *you*." Billy finally looked over at me. I felt a little relief when I saw that he wasn't glaring.

When I didn't say anything right away, Billy flung one hand up in the air. "Well, go on."

I swallowed. "I really like Blake a whole lot. I mean, I really, really do. He gets me, and I get him. It's a real thing."

"Why are you telling that to Billy?" Blake spoke. I turned my head to look at him and realized it might look weird that I just professed my feelings about him to Billy.

But I didn't hesitate. "Because he thinks I'm only dating you to piss off my family."

Blake frowned. I could hear Billy shift in his seat behind me, but I didn't look at him. I kept my attention on Blake. Blake put his half-eaten pizza back in the box. "Well, did you?"

"I don't think I did. At least not on purpose." I shot straight.

Blake frowned. "Well, are they pissed?"

"I haven't told them," I confessed.

Billy jumped up, grabbed his two pizza slices off the side of his chair, and walked over to sit on the carpet. His face was on the other side of the pizza box. "You haven't told them yet?" He was clearly surprised.

"Why?" Blake asked.

I took a deep breath. "Because if I told them and they got pissed, then Billy would be right. But if I didn't tell them, then Billy couldn't be right." Both of them were frowning, trying to make sense of my logic. "So I wanted to tell you both at the same time that I'm going to tell my parents, and I don't care how they react." I looked at Billy. "If they *are* upset, that doesn't make *you* right. I'm not the same girl I was in middle school." I felt my throat tighten. I didn't want to cry. Wasn't going to cry. "It wasn't right that I tried so hard to be friends with you to piss off my mother."

Blake's eyes opened wide as he looked at Billy and then back at me. "You did?"

"I'll explain later," I promised. "Point is that I'm not that same girl. But, I'm not sorry I did it."

"What?" Billy held up both hands that time.

"If I hadn't been that girl, then I wouldn't have found my best friend." As much as I hated it, I couldn't hold back my tears. "And I really miss my best friend."

Billy dropped his head to ruffle his brown curls. He always did that when he didn't want anyone to see him tear up. "You know you didn't have to shut me out. We could have figured it out together." He nodded his head toward Blake. "All three of us."

"Yeah, I know. But I didn't figure that out until today. I'm sorry." Something broke loose, and I sobbed. A good sob, like I had finally been able to let it all out. But there was no way I was making a habit of crying. Not a chance!

"Do I need to leave?" Blake asked. "Because I'm not getting this at all."

Both Billy and I started laughing through our tears. It must have looked and sounded crazy. Billy wiped his eyes on his sleeve and practically jumped over the coffee table to land on the other side of me. "No, Blake. If you like this crazy girl as much as she likes you, then you better stay. Because you'll learn a whole lot about her tonight. I'm a volume full of Emma Tang-Lee secrets."

"Oh, no, you don't!" I teased as I wiped my own face with Hancock Pizza napkins. "He may not want to date me anymore."

Blake's smile grew. "You both are crazy. BUT, if all this is about how much Emma likes me, then I'm in. But you've got a lot to explain."

Billy flung his arm around my neck. "Where do you want me to start?"

179

Chapter 47

1 a.m.

It was 1 a.m. before I headed home along 19th Street. I felt happy. It'd been a long time since I felt happy. As I was about to turn onto Grove Loop, my car's headlights caught someone walking a little further down the street. I recognized the green camo backpack, so I drove past my turn and headed straight for Lilly.

I tried to be sneaky and pull up slowly, but Lilly looked around a few times. She clearly couldn't tell who was following her since she suddenly started running. Her backpack bounced back and forth so hard that I thought she would fall over. I hated that she thought I was some creeper, so I sped up and caught up with her as soon as she reached Maple Street. I rolled down the window and screamed, "LILLY, IT'S ME!"

I'd never seen Lilly look so pale. She stood there panting. As soon as she caught her breath, she yelled, "WHY THE HELL ARE YOU FOLLOWING ME?"

"I wanted to make sure you're okay," I stated. That was half the truth. The other half was that I was trying to figure her out, but I wasn't telling her that.

Lilly walked over to my window. "I'm fine. Now leave."

"You tell me that a lot." I rolled my eyes, but I was ready to make things right with Lilly. I was on a roll. I'd left her in the belly of the pirate ship at the playground overnight and felt I'd made the wrong choice. This was my chance to make it right. "Can't you just let me help you?"

Lilly stared at me as she continued to calm her breathing. She didn't look thankful. In fact, she looked fed-up. She turned toward the house across the street from where I had pulled over. It was a small wooden house with a crooked porch. The windows were dark, and there was no car in the driveway. I wondered if that was her house, but I didn't dare ask after the look she had given me. She glanced back at me and asked, "How would you help me?"

I couldn't tell if she was being serious or if she was messing with me. "Well . . . I don't really know. Because I don't know how you need me to help." Even though her look hadn't changed, I still felt good about my answer.

Lilly leaned in, almost through the open window. Her backpack caught on the side, keeping her from moving in too far. It was too dark to see the color of her way-too-green eyes. Still, I could see her glaring

181

at me. "Look. I don't need you to keep trying to figure me out." So much for half-truths! She took a breath and forced a smile. "You seem nice and all, but I already have people looking out for me. I don't need more people in my business."

She wasn't being mean or angry. She was just over me butting into her life. "Like Zonta and Ozzie?" I asked. Those were the people she hung out with the most, along with some skinny, black freshman boy I didn't know at all.

Lilly nodded as she pulled her backpack off her shoulder and dropped it onto the sidewalk. Then she leaned back into my open car window. "Yeah. Like them."

Something didn't feel right so I decided to challenge her. "So are they okay with you sleeping in the playground at night?" I knew what half-truths looked like.

Lilly shrugged. "They don't know." She dropped her eyes before she added, "They don't need to know." Then she slowly looked back up at me. "Okay?"

I frowned. "No, not okay." Suddenly she wanted me to keep a secret like Blake was keeping one of her secrets. I shook my head. "You have to give me a little more than that!"

Lilly sighed. "Look." She pointed at the small house with the crooked porch. "That's where I live. I'll sleep there tonight."

"Why tonight and not on other nights?" I pushed.

"Because tonight it looks like I have the house to myself." She rolled her eyes and gave in. "When my aunt and her boyfriend are here, they party hard. So on those nights, I head to the pirate ship. But it's not every night. Sometimes they party somewhere else, and by this time, if they aren't back, then I know they won't be back until late sometime the next day or a few days later. My aunt always ends up giving me the play-by-play on how they passed out cold and hadn't been able to make it home. It's a pattern I'm getting used to." Lilly took in the frown on my face, so she quickly added, "But on those days that I sleep in the playground or somewhere else, I get to shower at the school."

I wasn't sure how to respond. I was in shock over how Lilly lived. How could she be so logical and calm about building her world around people who are either drunk or high *or* both? She was right. I had no idea how to help her. But she had said one thing that gave me hope. "So . . . the school knows about this?" I asked.

Lilly nodded. "Yes, they do."

A little part of me felt some relief. Was it because the burden was no longer mine? Or was she telling me a half-truth again? But I had seen her talking to Ms. Williams, who held her laptop for her. It explained why our teacher was never frustrated with Lilly being late. I had to believe Lilly was telling me the truth. "Okay." I looked at the dark house and then back at Lilly. "So you really are okay? Because it looks to me like you're a moth hurling yourself toward a flame."

Lilly gave me a small smile. "You said that to me once before." It was the first time she admitted to being the girl who slammed into me that cold night only three weeks earlier. "Well, tonight that flame is going to keep me warm." I raised my eyebrows. How could she be so calm? Lilly backed away from my car window and picked up her back pack. But before she left, she leaned down one more time and added. "Look, I really am okay." I nodded back at her. I wanted her to see that I believed her, even if it was hard to understand. She sighed but then quickly crossed the road and disappeared into the dark house.

Even though I didn't want to, I forced myself to accept Lilly's choice. I took a deep breath and turned my car around to head home.

Chapter 48

Glass of Water

I knocked on my parent's bedroom door. It was Wednesday night, and I knew I couldn't wait any longer. I had needed a few days, at least, to put my plan into play. I needed to see if I even had a chance at being heard. While Blake had worked Saturday and Sunday, I had studied Tammy's Biology notes carefully. She'd thankfully found someone who had filled in her missing details on the different kinds of cell transport, and her added side notes helped me too.

I had spent Monday and Tuesday, during the extra downtime in Chorus, going over questions I had with Mateo. He had promised he could study with me before school if I could get there early enough. He worked after school and had to rehearse with his own rock band after that. Early mornings were my only option. So I got out of bed and caught earlier buses to get to school by 7 a.m.

Wednesday morning's Biology exam had gone well. It was fed through the computer, so my results were instant. I'd made an 85. A solid B. I had a long way to go before any higher grades added up. But I realized I had a shot at getting a decent grade in Biology.

"Emma?" Ma cracked her door open. *"What's wrong?"* Her Mandarin was not more than a whisper.

"Ma, I need to talk to you," I responded in English.

"Okay." Ma opened the door all the way and let me follow her in. Ba was sitting up in bed reading. Ma climbed back into her side. I stopped at the foot of their bed but didn't sit down.

My heart was racing. How could I be so worried about talking to two sober parents? This wasn't like Lilly's world at all. But it was my world. I took a deep breath. The flames were mine to face, and I had learned from Blake that shooting straight was really my best chance at taking on the fire. A fire that I hadn't been able to put out by hoping it would just go away. "I am *not* going to take the SAT on Saturday."

Ba put down his book. *"But you already signed up—"*

"I know, and I will work extra hours in the store to pay you back for the cost." I didn't let them get a chance to argue with me. I dropped my eyes as I quickly explained. "I'm not ready. I haven't prepared." I looked up at them to see how they were taking the news. But they just sat there staring at me. "I'm sorry. I've been throwing a glass of water on a huge fire for some time now. But I promise you I have begun to try to save my grades at school."

186

"You have bad grades at school?" Ma asked. She looked confused.

I frowned. "You know I do. You get the report card in the mail."

Ma shook her head. *"I haven't seen any report cards since we moved to this address. They are still mailed to the store."* Ba shifted as Ma looked at him. *"Did you know this?"*

Ba shrugged. *"Yes. I read them and let you know she's okay."*

My mouth dropped open. Had my parents not even been worrying about me all this time? I didn't even know what to say, but Ma and Ba were not looking at me. Ma sat up straighter and stared at my father for a moment. When he didn't add any more insight, she let out a loud grunt. *"But she's not okay. It looks like she has not been okay for a long time."* Great! If she hadn't been worried before, she suddenly had reason to be. I began to think that maybe my shooting straight had made things worse.

Ba shook his head. *"She's okay."* He pointed at me. *"See! She's making good decisions on her own."*

Ma barely glanced at me. *"Maybe now! But maybe it's too late!"* Ma raised her voice. Not in anger but in worry. I couldn't figure out what move I could make that would help, so I just stood there and kept my mouth shut.

Ba reached over and patted his wife's arm. *"It's never too late. If we had pushed Emma to do it our way, then it would have been like asking a fox for its skin."* He shook his head. *"Emma must do it her way."* Then he grinned at me. *"Like tonight."*

Ma looked over at me, trying to figure me out. My throat tightened, and I didn't even try to keep my tears from falling. Then I said the one thing that I couldn't hold down any longer. "I'm sorry I'm not as perfect as Joe."

Ma shook her head. *"I don't know what you're talking about."*

"You're always celebrating him." I pointed out as I tried to wipe my tears with the back of my hand.

"He has many things to celebrate." She looked at Ba, who was suddenly stone-faced. This wasn't the first time they'd discussed this topic. She looked back at me. *"We will celebrate you when you have something to celebrate."* She nodded. *"Okay?"*

I shook my head. "Whatever." I was over it all. I had said what I had to say. I didn't feel better, but I wasn't holding everything in anymore. Even though nothing had changed, at least they knew what was really going on. Except, there was one more thing I hadn't told them yet. Blake.

"You don't speak to me that way." Ma started to reprimand me. But Ba touched her shoulder, so she stopped.

"Maybe it's a good idea to go to sleep," Ba suggested.

Ma nodded. I had been dismissed. As I headed for their door, I stopped. I wasn't leaving their room holding onto one more secret that they may not like. So I turned back around. "By the way, I'm dating Blake Dockins. He has autism, and his father has nothing to do with him. He's good to me, and he gets me. I'm not asking for permission. I'm just telling you."

I shut the door and went to my room. I could hear my parents continue to argue in hushed tones. It didn't go at all as I had hoped, but I knew that at least Ba had a clue about what made me tick. As I stood in the darkness of my room, I realized that I felt a little lighter. To be real, even though I was working hard to change, I had just given my mother a reason to think less of me. But it was on her now, not me.

Chapter 49

Special

The knock on my door was strong. It was Saturday morning. I rolled over in bed and pulled my covers over my head. A second knock made me sit up. "What is it, Ma?"

Ma opened the door. *"It's time to get up."*

"I told you I am not taking the test!" I flopped back down. She was too much. We had hardly spoken in three days, but it was more like she was avoiding me. I watched Ba give her looks, but Ma would just frown and head to the kitchen. Then there were still the hushed-late-night arguments coming from my parents' room. I had no idea why she thought she could push me to take the test after all that went down.

"I made a special appointment for you at Hancock Hair." Ma said as if this was as normal as eating dinner. Except, she put emphasis on the word *special*.

I sat up. "What are you talking about?" I couldn't wrap my head around what she had said.

Ma smiled a little. Just like that, there it was! She was trying. After three days of hardly talking to me, she was trying to move on. *"I know you like to dye your hair and it looks like the color is fading."*

My mouth dropped. I knew she didn't like my dyed low lights, but I also knew that this was my mother's way of trying to make things between us right. She would never say she was sorry. She couldn't. But she was trying in her own way. Once, in middle school, she had ruined my favorite shirt in the wash. When I came home from school, I found a fruit basket on my desk with a gift certificate to a clothing store. It had been a long time since she thought she was in the wrong.

I wanted to cry with relief, but I didn't want to scare her away, so I smiled at her instead. I cleared my throat and spoke Mandarin for the first time in years. *"Thank you. That would be very nice."*

Chapter 50

Real

I stretched out on a wide metal beam next to the gym. It was Monday after school, and Blake had asked me to wait for him while he had some meeting with Coach Miller and the rest of the team. They were taking official pictures to blow up and mount along Hancock High's gym hallway.

I was wearing my favorite red crop-top blouse and jeans that had enough rips to show parts of my legs. I had my back against the cool beam, and my bare skin enjoyed the warmth of the spring day. As I rested my arm over my eyes as I waited, I suddenly realized that I felt peaceful. It had been a long time. I looked forward to taking the bus with Blake to his place. We promised his mother we would watch Penny while she worked and I hoped I'd finally get to meet Blake's brother, Kyle, too.

"You look hot!" Chastity startled me. I jerked my arm away from my eyes to stare at her. She'd braided her long, wavy hair to one side.

"What?" I asked. Her light green eyes had that look that meant she was up to something. "Are you hitting on me?" I teased as I sat up. It was the first time I didn't want to scream at her. Let's be real, she was annoying, but I didn't have a reason to be angry with her. I smiled to myself. I was figuring this anger thing out and happy that I hadn't taken a headache pill in two days. That was long for me. I hadn't realized how many pills I took in a day until I enjoyed two days without them.

She jumped up onto the beam to sit next to me. "Even though it is tempting, I think I'll stick with Owen."

"What do you want from me, Chastity?" I finally asked her. I watched the tone of my voice, but I still shot straight. "You keep getting into my business and pushing your . . . whatever it is you and Owen have . . . onto me. Onto Blake and me." I shook my head but said as a matter of fact, "It's got to stop."

When she didn't come back with a snide comment, I turned to look at her. Her smirk was gone, and she looked upset. "You really think I'm getting into your business?" I nodded, but I felt a little sorry for the girl who was showing way more skin than I was. She pulled her short dress down toward her knees. We sat in silence for a few minutes before she spoke again. "I suck at it, you know?"

I looked over at her again. "At what?"

193

"Having girlfriends." She jerked her head toward the gym door. "Owen is great, but I get tired of hanging with his friends. I thought you and Blake meant I'd finally have a girl who would hang with us. A girl who was like me."

My mouth dropped. "Like you?" I held my tongue. I was nothing like her, but I didn't want to make her feel worse. I felt my shoulders tense, so I focused on dropping them. I would not get a headache. I was not going to let Chastity ruin my two-day streak.

"Yeah." She smiled gently. "Alone."

It hit me. Hard. She was right. Except for Billy, I had been alone. All the girls who sat with us at lunch were his friends, not mine. Then there was Lilly, who I was trying to be friends with. At least, that was what I thought was happening. But she told me straight-up that she wanted me to butt out of her life.

Except, at that moment, I had to be real with myself. I didn't only have Billy anymore—I had Blake and Zonta and Ozzie. Then there was Mateo and his wise-ass comments. Ones that made me think. Of course, my parents and Joseph had never thought I was a lesser-Tang-Lee. I just never knew it . . . not until I learned to shoot straight. Learned to be real. My world was changing. A little.

I felt my shoulders relax as I gave Chastity a smile. "I've never really been alone." Then I laughed out loud. "I just pushed almost everyone around me away. There is a difference."

Chastity nodded. Then she looked me right in the eyes. "Are you going to push me away?"

I took a deep breath. "It depends."

"On what?"

"If you can stop making everything about sex and hooking up. That's not my world. At all. So you're going to have to find something else to talk about." Chastity nodded a she lifted her head up and let the sun warm her face. I waited and waited. "Well, what else can you talk about?"

Chastity looked at me and said with a little sass, "Give me some time. I'm thinking!"

I burst out laughing.

Laughing felt good.

Acknowledgements

Writing *Emma* could never have happened without the help of several individuals. A special thanks to all of the following people who played a role in the process. I am forever grateful to each of you for the time and support you provided. Your engagement in the story and responses to the characters inspire me to continue on this journey into the world of Hancock High.

To my parents Jonlyn and G. Keith Parker, who were willing to take on the first read-through of the manuscript *and* multiple additional drafts. They have not only embraced the characters' lives with gusto, but they have shown unwavering support for the whole writing process. To Ben Onachila, who also was willing to take on the first read-through and provide me with refreshing feedback. His uncanny poetic ability has helped me iron out some rough edges. To my daughters, Maya Borhaug and Sarah Borhaug, whose read-throughs helped me keep the story and characters real. To Kym Sebranek, Sheila Mooney, José Rene Perez, Michael Bower, Mary Ann Galyon and Dr. Tara P. Bacote for reading through the manuscript and providing valuable feedback, each bringing their unique perspective to the table, supporting my desire to provide an authentic story. To Nastia Parker for guiding me through the intricate world of social media and texting trends and her willingness to model for the cover.

Many thanks to Hanna Yau for dialoguing with me at length and to Shutao Wang, who read through the manuscript and gracefully suggested needed changes to make sure I represented the Chinese - American culture accurately.

For direction and guidance concerning wrestling I would like to thank Vernon Bryson, Jimmy Jones, Hayden Davis Hooper, and Carlo Colombo. A special thanks to Elijah Eubanks for reviewing and editing wrestling sections.

Thanks to Renee Roof, Barbara Grimm and Olivia Shuler for their insight into teen homelessness. My daughter, Amy Borhaug, who whispers words of perseverance and courage. Nioca Robinson, whose encouragement I dearly value.

My copy editor Julie Overpeck, who not only understands the importance of Hi-Lo books, but helped turn out a professional product. A special thanks to Transylvania County Schools and Brevard High School for the use of their property for the cover shot.

Sarah Borhaug's time, commitment, creativity and professional skill in shooting, editing and designing the cover are deeply appreciated.

Last but not least, my husband, Tore, for his unwavering support and his steady grounding. Without him, none of it would be possible.

Emma's Text/Slang/Terms

The following are definitions of how terms are used in *Emma*. Some terms may have other definitions that are not included.

2—to, too, two

4—four, for

abt—about

ACT—American College Testing, a test used by colleges and universities to measure how ready a student is for college or university. ACT scores are used by the colleges and universities to compare students. This is often one factor used to help decide who should be admitted.

fireman's carry—in wrestling, when the wrestler moves into their opponent and manages to roll them over their shoulder and land the opponent with their back against the mat

k—okay

light rail—an above-ground train

luv—love

nvm—nevermind

relic—an object that is very old but also tells something about the past

SAT—a test used by colleges and universities to measure how ready a student is for college or university. SAT scores are used by the colleges and universities to compare students. This is often one factor used to help decide who should be admitted.

sick—1. awful 2. awesome, cool

sux—sucks

tbh—to be honest

thnx—thanks

throw shade—say something slightly disrespectful

transit—local transportation

ttyl—talk to you later

u—you

ur—you're, your

wench—an old word for a young woman, but can also mean prostitute

wup—what's up?

y—why?

yt—you there?